Crazy DéJà Vu

Part 2

"Not Again"

By
Lauresa Tomlinson

Copyright

2019

Young of Heart Pub

P.O. Box 2274

Mckinleyville, CA

95519

Dedication

I dedicate this 2nd part to my fans. I hope this one answers all of your questions and sets your mind's at ease.
Smiles to all of you.

Crazy DéJà vu
part two
"Not again"

Chapter One

Now I am really caught in a science fiction life and there are only a few people I can talk to about what is really happening.

As time has passed, I have learned a lot about painting. But I have this feeling that there is a little something that I am missing. And as time gets closer for me to move to SF I am feeling a little unsure about the whole thing.

I won't know anyone there and I will only have Nell to talk to because Jack isn't allowed to use the phones.

Jack and I have remained in contact and have become really good friends over the last few years. At least once a week we manage to meet and talk about things. And I often find myself wondering what changes my actions were making for Anna, my future self.

I haven't asked Jack but I don't think there is a way to communicate with Anna. I mean like sending a message to find out what has changed for her. Next time I meet up with Jack I think I will ask about that.

Time seems to be moving faster for me and I only have about another six months before I go to San Francisco and find and meet Master Bastrono.

I was planning to have a few sidewalk sales before moving and found out yesterday that my new friends (Janis and Fred) that moved into 4A were planning to have one next month for extra summer cash. We decided to join efforts and have even a larger sale.

I was sorting through things to make it a little easier on myself to move when the time came and figured a few extra dollars could come in handy. While going through a few boxes at the bottom of my closet I found a notebook with a pretty but strange picture on the front cover. The title on the first page was "When I get the time and money I want to…"

And on that page, I had written –
1. "I want to learn how to paint"
2. "I want to visit and maybe live in S.F. CA"
3. "I want to see the Pacific Ocean"
4. "I want to make enough money to travel".

But a question started nagging at the back of my mind. *'Would I have wanted to paint or see the Pacific Ocean if Anna hadn't come back. Yet here, right now in front of me was the answer. These were things that I had written down in the past. Things I was thinking about. OR was this a book that Anna had planted here for me to find. But on second thought, how would she have known when I was going to look in this box. Oh duh, she must have known my every move, after all, she had already done these things.'*

Ouch, all this is doing is giving me a headache. I really need to find things I know I won't be using or haven't used in years to put in the sidewalk sale.

I found a pencil and wrote at the bottom of the page. **"If you find that you have to be in control. Don't travel through time!"**

While I was looking through all the other things in the box and separating the ones for the sale, my mind was coming up with questions to ask Jack next time we were together.

For instance. *'When you travel through time, how do you know that you are really traveling back to the right dimension and not crossing into another time frame. I mean I think we live in several time frames at the same time and that is why we have déjà vu and we have fears of things like spiders, water or heights. Maybe we almost died of a spider bite in another area or we almost drowned or fell off something high and got hurt. Who knows? It doesn't seem like it would take much for the vibration streams to be off a little and we would cross into a different reality.'*

These kinds of thoughts are enough to make one's head swirl but I keep going back to them. *'I wonder if these thoughts are cleared up in the future.'*

I remember being at Nell's house playing when we were little and hearing her mom and dad talking about such things, but didn't pay much attention then. They were both research scientists in quantum physics. I still don't understand exactly what that is. But I think that is why I feel I can talk to Nell about anything especially the strange things that happen to me.

For her this kind of brainstorming (as she calls it) and thinking is normal.

As for my dad, he was a chess Master and always said life is like playing chess. "You always need to plan a few moves in all directions before making a move." Mom just said "That means you need to plan ahead when possible" translating it for me at the time.

My dad died about four months after my twelfth birthday but mom and I managed to stay living in the same block.

Nell and I have been best friends since preschool.

About a year after my mom died, her parents moved to Texas for their retirement. Nell managed to stay in their apartment, while I moved down the street to one I could afford.

Jack and I have made it a point to get together at least every Wednesday for the past few years. I have managed to get him talked into watching a movie with me every few weeks and eating somewhere else other than the Roster Café.

Today is Tuesday and I seriously need to keep my mind on this if I am going to have all of the sales items together in two weeks.

I have managed to paint a few pictures over the past few years. I wonder if I should put them out for sale. I did like said Jack said and signed all of them A.M. Stolks. I wonder if people will remember all of the talk about Anna's painting from years ago?

Time pasted and Janis, Fred and I piled all of our things out onto the sidewalk after putting up signs everywhere we could find a place to hang them. I even hung one of them at the Roster Café.

Everything was going really good until a man came by and saw my paintings and asked if I was the painter and not thinking I said yes. I am the one who painted them but they were signed A.M. Stolks. And of course, the signature was the same.

"I don't think you are the same person I am thinking of. I met the real A.M. Stolks." He said.

"Where did you meet her?" I asked.

"She stayed at the Clair Mont Hotel." He said rather rudely.

"Yes, on the 2nd floor, Mandy was the floor maid that took care of all of her needs and Danny the bellhop would run special errands. My hair was lighter then." I said with a smile.

"My sister lived here and I am helping her out today," I added. "Are you interested in buying one of my paintings?" I continued raising one eyebrow.

"Oh, I am sorry for my rudeness. Yes, I am interested. How much are you asking for this small painting of the meadow? He asked holding up the small 8x11 inch painting.

"I am asking $500 for that one," I said in my strongest sounding voice.

"Will you take a check?" he asked.

"Do you have an ID?" I asked.

"Yes, mam." He said pulling out his wallet.

I looked at the name 'Rudolf Beaterman'. Now I remember hearing that name called when I went to see Anna. I think he was in maintenance.

"Rudolf, were you in maintenance at the Clair Monte Hotel?" I asked.

"Yes mam, I was." He said pulling out his checkbook.

"Ok, but write the check out to my sister Rita Stolks." I informed him.

"Ok, here it is. Thank you. I am so proud. I now have a painting by Miss Anna." He said with a large smile as he walked away holding it up.

Janis looked over at me and said. "I thought your name is Rita?" she questioned.

"It is but I paint as Anna M. Stolks. That way I don't have to do a lot of explaining as to the way I live or where I live and it keeps away all of the news hunters. I went through all of that a while back." I said, "But shhh don't tell anyone. Okay?" I said.

"Sure we can keep a secret." She said with a smile and Fred nodded in agreement.

Although that was the only painting I sold, I did manage to get rid of a lot of other things that I really didn't need anymore. Janis and Fred sold almost everything they had for sale. I only had three other paintings.

"So not a bad day after all, how did you two do?" I asked just out of curiosity.

"Not bad at all. We sold almost everything we had out. We were both wondering," Janis looked over at Fred and he nodded. "What is the lowest cost painting you have to sell?"

"Well since we live in the same building and I can't take everything with me, how about $100 for your choice," I said holding up the three small paintings I had left. One was of a farmhouse, one of a stream with apple trees, and one of an old house with fenced yard and a flowering arbor with a half-opened gate.

"I like the old house," Janis said, looking over at Fred. He smiled "Yes. Deal." He said holding out the money.

Chapter Two

Just as Fred handed me the money Anna caught my attention by meowing from the window above me. I had left the window open so she could see me through the screen and know I was still close by.

I took the last two paintings and headed upstairs.

"Hi baby girl," I said as I opened the door.

She ran past me from the bedroom where she had been in the window, watching to the kitchen meowing the whole way.

I had to laugh at the sound she was making. "Ok I said I am coming," I said placing the paintings on the couch.

"Oh I see, you have cleaned your bowl so well I don't think I will have to wash it tonight," I said going to get her some milk.

"Well baby girl, I think we are getting pretty close to having enough money to go to San Francisco," I said sitting down at the table and taking the money out of my pockets.

Anna had to come and investigate

when she heard the change dropping and rolling across the table, she came running, jumped up on the other chair and managed to catch a nickel under her paw before it could roll off the table.

"Good catch pretty girl," I said stroking across the shoulders and back.

I rolled a few pennies in her direction while I counted the change, then I got up and grabbed a pencil and paper off the counter to write down the amounts as I counted them. I wanted to be able to see just what was made from the sales today.

Anna was getting as much fun out of catching the coins as I was rolling them to her. So far she had only missed one.

"Not too bad Anna. We made $782.53 today." I announced.

And she replied with a long drawn out meow. As if to say is that all?"

"Well, we didn't really have all that much to sell today,." I said trying to shore up my side of this conversation as I laughed.

"I think I need to find out just what it will cost us to fly to San Francisco CA this summer. That is when things usually get a little slower at The Rooster. Come to think about it, there really hasn't been a slow time since Anna's painting. But still, I think the summer would be a good time to go see what S.F has to offer us.

It's been a busy morning and I think I am going to go see Nell. It's almost two o'clock and she should be getting home on

George's next run.

'Looking through the frig with Anna wrapping herself around my legs is ok until I get ready to move.' I thought with a chuckle.

"Baby girl, do you want a corn dog for lunch?" I asked showing it to her.

She was quick to answer with a "Meow" and both paws went up the side of the frig.

"I guess that is a strong yes," I said laughing.

I turned to get them ready for the microwave and almost stepped on Anna's tail.

"Anna! Get on the chair so I don't step on you." I commanded, then went back to prepare the corndogs for the microwave.

She made a quick jump to the chair then stood up on her hind legs and looked over the back of it at what I was doing.

When I turned to see what she was doing I had to laugh. "You know sometimes I think you are trying to become a human. It wouldn't surprise me if one of these days you make your own lunch."

I set the timer then got the milk out and put some in her bowl.

That caught her attention and she jumped down and was at her bowl like lightening.

I went in and turned on the TV. I wasn't sure what was on because I was usually at work by this time on Tuesday. But Charlie had given me the week off. He said it was my vacation. I asked him if it was with pay since I had worked for him so many years and he laughed and said, "Well let me think about that one." And that is all I got from him. I guess I will find out when I go back to work next week.

There isn't anything worth watching on TV Anna. So I think after we eat lunch we will listen to the radio while I go through my drawers to see what I want to take on our trip to San Francisco.

I put our plates in the sink and ran water on them then I went to the bedroom with Anna on my heels.

I turned on the radio and they were playing some lively music that made me want to dance. I guess it made Anna feel the same way. Because when I looked over at her, she was on the bed, prancing. With her feet being lifted high off the bed like a parade horse. Then she turned and bowed with her head almost touching the bed then started all over again.

"I didn't know you knew how to dance. You are amazing." I said watching her then making a few turns of my own.

At the end of the song, she made one last bow then turned over on her back and kicked all four paws in the air as if she was running fast.

I had to laugh. "You are sure a great friend," I said sitting on the bed and petting her.

Anna got up and ran for the door. I got

up to follow and about the time I got to the bedroom door I hear the knock.

"Who could be at my door' I wondered as I heard the knock again.

"Who is it?" I asked listening for the reply.

"It's Nell."

I opened the door and sure enough, it was Nell.

"I got off a little early so I thought I would come to your house this time," she said laughing as she walked over and sat down on the couch.

"Should I put on a pot of water?" I asked

"No, you can come over here so we can talk," she said looking up at me.

I was a little surprised to see her at my house and found myself still standing at with the door open.

I closed the door and walked over to the couch and sat down while saying "okay".

Just as I sat down Anna jumped onto the couch between us and meowed as if to say she wanted to be part of whatever was going on.

What's up?" I asked.

"Oh not much. I got off early and thought I would drop in to see you for a change." Nell announced. "But I do want to know what is happening?" she quizzed with a big grin.

"What do you mean?" I asked.

"Well, I know that you met Jack a few

years ago and that he has been coming to eat at the Rooster at least once a week. Are you talking more often now? Or what?" Nell asked, almost chuckling to herself.

"Yes, in the last six months he has gotten his boss to let him off duty twelve hours a week. When I first met Jack he was only off duty long enough to run to the grocery store once a week. So what was your question again?" I asked laughing.

"Are you two dating yet?" Nell asked point-blank.

"If you can call it that. During his twelve hours off, we go to eat a meal together and then go to the grocery store. Then sometimes if there is time and something worth watching we manage to see a movie. But the movie watching so far has been about twice a month. I do have to say he is fun to talk to. I really like him a lot. But I'm not real sure how he feels about me." I explained.

"So what's going to happen after you move to San Francisco?" asked Nell, looking a little more serious.

"I don't know. I try not to think about that. It makes me a little sad, but I guess it is something I have to do or there wouldn't be a reason for any of this to have happened." I said.

"Well, what's on TV tonight? Nell asked, changing the subject.

"I'm really not sure. I didn't pick up a schedule this week." I said with a cheesy smile.

"Flip it on and let's find out. Or I guess it is early enough to go to watch a movie." Nell said.

"You know there is one movie I hear people talking about at the Rooster the other day and it sounded pretty interesting," I said.

"What's the title and where is it playing do you know?" Nell asked.

"The Fifth Realm is playing at the little cinema two blocks east of here," I said looking at the paper.

"Oh, I heard that is a good movie. Let's go see that one. What time does it start?" Nell asked.

I looked at my watch. "It starts in about forty-five minutes. If we leave now we can take our time getting there." I said.

Then I caught sight of Anna trying to keep up with the conversation. First looking at Nell and then me, it was as if she was watching a tennis match. I had to laugh while picking her up and giving her a hug. "You are just so cute," I said.

"Nell and I are going to see a movie and I will be home a little later," I said while putting a little more food in her dish and grabbing my jacket. "Now you be a good girl."

I turned on the TV and made sure the remote was on the couch near her mouse.

Nell gave me a funny look.

"She knows how to change the

channels," I said while laughing at the odd look Nell just gave me.

Checking my pocket, I made sure I had my keys and wallet. "Ok, I'm ready to go," I said while opening the door.

"It's a nice night for a walk,." Nell said after about a block with no conversation. "You are really quiet tonight. What's going on?" she questioned.

"Oh, I was just thinking about the move to San Francisco. That's a big move and a lot of changes all of a sudden." I said, looking down as we walked along.

"What changes are troubling you?" Nell asked.

"I have lived in this same area all of my life. We went all the way through school together. And you have always been them for me to talk to." I said trying not to cry. "I miss all of this already and I haven't even moved yet,." I added.

"Now not to worry about all of that, I will be as close as a phone call. You know that I will be there for you when you need me. We have always been there for each other. After all I don't think there are very many people that would know what we are talking about." She said with a chuckle and a big smile as she reached over and gave me a hug.

"That is true," I said and we laughed the rest of the way to the show.

"I get to pay for the tickets tonight and you can buy the popcorn and drinks. Okay?"

I said hoping for Nell to agree.

"Okay, that sounds pretty even to me." she laughed.

"So was the movie about what you thought it would be?" Nell asked laughing.

"Hum, well let me think. I guess a little of it could play out but I am hoping that the big cities don't look like that in the future." I said, trying not to laugh. "What do you think?" I questioned.

"I don't think that the aliens will look much like that, at least the ones that designed the building in the movie," Nell said trying not to laugh. "It is hard to have a serious conversation about that movie," she added as we continued walking back to my apartment.

"That is true," I said and she joined me in full laughter. "But that was fun," I added.

We picked up the pace as the wind caught a slight chill.

"It must be getting ready to rain," I said.

"Why do you say that?" questioned Nell.

"Because the temp just got cooled," I said with a smile.

"True, I don't know what I was thinking just now," Nell said starting to laugh again. "Have you and Jack had a chance to see many movies." she quizzed.

Chapter Three

"No. Not really. We saw this one last week. But most of our time is taken up talking and shopping," I informed her.

It just started a light sprinkle as we got to my steps.

"You need to come up and take my red umbrella home with you so you don't get wet," I said looking over at Nell still standing on the sidewalk, holding tight to her sweater.

"Okay," she said almost running up the steps to the door.

As I unlocked my door, I heard a thump from inside. I knew that Anna would be at the door waiting for me to come in.

"Watch Anna is at the door waiting to greet me," I said turning to Nell.

As we saw her we both gave out a giggle.

"Hello baby girl. What did you watch on TV while we were gone?" I asked looking over at the TV.

She had managed to find a channel

with animals. "Now that is a good channel to watch," I said petting her.

Nell was standing almost behind me. She put her hand on my shoulder. "Umbrella?" she said.

As I turned around she gave me a big Cheshire grin and I had to laugh.

I reached over behind the couch and pulled out a bright red umbrella. "Here you go. This should keep you dry on your way home. But the news is just starting are you sure you don't want to stay long enough to hear it?" I questioned.

"No, that is quite alright I have a few things I need to get done before I go to bed tonight," she said turning towards the door.

"Okay then. I will see you on the bus tomorrow morning. But not after work." I said opening the door.

"Why is that?" she asked.

"Because. Jack and I have things to do this Wednesday. He gets his twelve hours off tomorrow." I explained while standing at the door with her.

"Ooooh, Okay. Then I will see you in the morning then," she said with a chuckle as she walked down the stairs.

I closed the door and looked over at the TV as Anna let out a long meow. There was a program about lions on. "Of that is great a story about your cousins," I said with a chuckle as I sat down near her.

Next commercial we both decided it was time to get something to eat. Anna was already standing in front of the frig as I entered the kitchen. Well, aren't you the fast one tonight," I said. "Let's get something quick so we can watch the rest of the lions," I said putting her food in her bowl.

She ate some then ran back in and jumped up on the couch while I grabbed my sandwich and joined her.

After that program, we watch the next one about birds. I had to laugh as she reached out in their direction then acted like she was stretching. It was getting late and morning would come early enough.

"I think its lime to get in bed," I said as that program ended and I turned off the TV. She jumped down and ran back into the kitchen. I grabbed the book I had started and walked to the bedroom. By the time I got into bed and got set up to read a little, she came running in meowing as she ran, then onto the bed she jumped. She played with her mouse a little while I read a little then I turned off the light and we both fell asleep quickly.

The morning sun was shining brightly through the lower half on the bedroom window. It seems that the rain had passed us during the night

The bed started to shake and the windows started to rattle. Anna looked over at me and gave a long "Meeoow"

"Yes that was an earthquake, I'm pretty sure," I said looking at Anna.

Then the phone rang. "Did you feel that at your house?" Nell said almost yelling with excitement. "Is everything ok there?" she asked.

"Yes, as far as I know." Then came the aftershock, a loud thud, and rumble before I could say anything else. The phone went dead and the light in the bathroom went off.

"Oh my! Anna this may be a little more involved than I thought earlier," I said getting dressed quickly and picking up Anna.

I walked slowly and as lightly as I knew how across the floor to the door. We lived in one of the older building and I wasn't sure what the thud was I had heard earlier.

I opened the door just enough to peek through a crack, then slowly opened it all the way. That is when I noticed that where the large hanging light globe used to hang was now empty. "The light must have broken loose during the quake and rolled down the stairs," I told Anna who was very satisfied being held. "Maybe that is what we heard that rumbled," I added.

"Meow," Anna said in what I took as agreeing.

I slowly tiptoed to the top of the stairs and there I could see that one of the ceiling beams had fallen across the stairwell.

"Oh my Anna, it looks like we may be stuck here for a while unless we can crawl under that beam. But I don't think that would be safe. I wonder what the rest of the building looks like." I said.

"Meow," said Anna as if to agree.

I placed Anna on the floor beside me and took two steps to the edge of the stair casing to look over the edge to the main floor. "Oh My!"

"Meow" Anna seemed to ask with both paws on my leg.

I picked her up and we both looked over the edge.

There was glass, a couple of beams and plenty of plaster. It looked like the last four steps were missing. I turned and looked up towards the sixth floor just in time to dodge another piece of plaster and then noticed that the sidewall from the stairs was missing from the fifth floor.

Just then my attention turned back towards the main floor. RITA! RITA! Came a familiar voice.

"NELL! IS THAT YOU?" I yelled as loud as I could.

By this time Mary from next door had stuck her head out of her door. "Is it safe out there?" she asked.

"I don't know how much damage is done below. So it may be safer in your room. Just walk softly and the least amount as you can. Leave your door open so you can hear what is happening." I instructed.

"Okay, thanks," she said standing there for a few more minutes.

I really didn't want anyone else standing where I was because I didn't know how much damage there was to the area I was now standing in.

"YES! Are YOU OKAY?" Nell yelled.

"YES, CAN YOU CALL FOR HELP. THE PHONES ARE OUT AND THERE IS NO ELECTRIC. SO BE CAREFUL." I yelled down to her.

I could make out a long shadow in the doorway. The sun was shining just right for me to tell it was Nell. The shadow was now leaving.

Just then I heard Janis from the 4th floor above me. "What damage do you see Rita?"

"Well there are parts of the stairs that are missing and at least one ceiling bean that has come loose, the electric and phones are out. What are you seeing up there?" I said loudly.

"Part of the ceiling in our bedroom fell and a piece hit Fred on the back. But he is ok as far as I can tell. Outside of a cracked window and a few broken dishes, we are okay." she said almost being drowned out by the fire engines and police sirens.

"We should have plenty of help soon," I said.

"RITA! JERRY HERE." Jerry is a fireman I know.

"YES, I'M HERE," I yelled back watching the shadows move in the doorway below.

"ARE YOU OK AND WHAT ABOUT THE OTHERS ON YOUR FLOOR?" he called out.

"I'M OK AND I HAVE ONLY SEEM MARRY. SHE IS LOOKING AT ME FROM HER DOOR. I'M NOT TO SURE HOW SAFE IT IS TO WALK AROUND. I DON'T THINK BILL IS HOME YET. HE WORKS GRAVEYARD. JOE AND NANCY STARTED THEIR VACATION YESTERDAY AND I DON'T THINK THEY ARE HOME." I said trying to talk loud enough to be heard over all of the commotion downstairs.

"THANK YOU," he said

A larger shadow came to the door Tim's voice boomed over the bullhorn. "THE ELECTRIC AND GAS ARE NOW TURNED OFF. SO IF YOU ARE ABLE, PLEASE WALKS SOFTLY AND SLOWLY TO YOUR FRONT DOOR AND STAND IN THE DOORWAY AND WAIT FOR HELP. DO NOT TRY TO EXIT THIS BUILDING WITHOUT OUR HELP AS IT IS UNSAFE. PARTS OF THE STAIRS ARE MISSING AND WE ARE NOT SURE AT THIS POINT HOW SAFE THE HALLWAYS ARE." he instructed.

"MARK AND JUDY ARE OK" Janis reported

"Lonie shouted from the sixth floor. "JOYCE BROKE HER LEG DURING THE QUAKE."

Just then Baker and a new fireman came through the front window down the hall on my floor. "We are taking everyone from the building by ladder, one floor at a time," Baker told Mary. While they were helping her I went back to my apartment and grabbed my jacket. My wallet and keys were already in the pocket.

It was soon my turn to go down the ladder. Anna didn't want to be held so she perched on my shoulder on the way down.

Nell had gone home and brought back her camera and was taking pictures. She met me as I got off the ladder.

"I got the cutest picture of Anna perched on your shoulder," she said. "Would you like to see it?" she asked with a light giggle.

"Sure," I said petting Anna to calm her down, then I tucked her inside my jacket.

Jerry walked up about that time. "Hi Nell, I saw you taking pictures. Did you get any good shots of the rescues?" he asked.

"I think I got a few good ones," Nell replied.

"Can I take a look at what you have?" he asked reaching for the camera.

"Well, Rita hasn't seen them yet either. Why don't you come around here and look at them with us?" she offered.

"Okay sounds good," he said making his way in back of us.

"Oh Anna, you are so cute. I want a copy of that one for the firehouse," he said.

"I agree, I want one too," I said with a chuckle.

"Oh yeah, you got a few good ones. I think the newspaper may buy them from you," he said with a big grin.

"Well I have to get back to what is needed," he said with a small wave as he left.

"It looks like I will need a place to stay for a few days," I said hinting to Nell.

"Of course, You know my door is always open to you and Anna. I don't think they will let anyone back into this place for a while," Nell said with a smile.

"I just happen to think I hope I can get a few things out of my apartment that I will need soon," I said looking around for Baker (The captain).

"BAKER" I yelled waving my hands.

"I need to go talk to him. I will be back in a few minutes," I said making my way through the crowd that had gathered to watch all of the excitement.

Chapter Four

"Baker, there are a few things I need from my apartment. Is there a way to get them today?" I asked.

"After the crow and excitement dies down then I can send one of the men back in to get what you need," he said.

"Okay thanks," I said then I turned to Nell and gave a big grin. She started to walk towards me to find out what was happening.

"What was all of that about?" she quizzed.

"DO you remember the envelope that Anna gave me?" I asked.

"Yes," she said in a questioning tone.

"Well, I don't want to take a chance on it getting lost. So I asked and I think that Baker will let Jerry go back to my apartment after all of this is pretty much over and get everything from my top drawer. If he gets all of the contents then no one will know just what it was that was so important," I explained.

"Oh, good thinking," Nell said.

We went and sat on the steps next door so as not to be in the way and watched for what seemed like a very long time.

"I don't think this place will be livable for a while and my rent was due in a few days. I will give that money to you instead," I said. "That way I don't get out of the habit of paying rent."

Then Jerry walked up. "Now just what was it that you needed from your apartment right away?" he asked.

"I need everything that is in the top drawer of the tall dresser in my bedroom. Can you get all of that for me please?" I asked with begging prayer hands, and a smile.

"Sure. It's okay if I put it all in a plastic bag right?" he asked. "I have some in the cab of the truck," he added.

"Sure, just be careful not to lose anything," I said with a big smile.

"I won't I will be careful," he said. "You know me well enough not to worry about that," he added.

"True." And all three of us laughed.

He had things that his mom gave him when he was four years old. He said they were important to him. I knew I could trust him.

Soon he came back down the ladder with a white kitchen trash bag about half full. "Here is everything that was in that drawer including a few stray bobby pins. I just turn the drawer upside down in the bag," he said with a hardy laugh.

"Thank you," I said as I stepped closer to

him and took it from his hand as he held it out.

"Let me know when I can get in and gather other things. Oh, you did lock my door right?" I asked as a second thought.

"Yes we locked everyone's apartment and yes we will let all of you know when it is safe to go in and get other things. We just need to know where you will be so we can contact you," he informed me.

"I will be staying with Nell for at least a few days anyway," I said.

"What did you have planned today besides going to work?" Nell asked. "Which I may tell you now, you are late doing," she said looking at her watch. "Let's head for my house and you can call Charlie from there," she added.

"Good idea." I agreed.

"First I need to check the bag for a few things," I said, as I sat down on the steps nearby.

"Oh good, everything is here," I said with a sigh of relief.

"You need to call Charlie," Nell reminded me.

"Oh yeah. Today is a real shaker," I said with a chuckle.

As soon as we got to Nell's house I called Charlie.

"Hello, Charlie?" I said as he answered the phone.

"Rita! Why aren't you at work?" he said in a voice he used when he knew what was going on and wanted to sound tough.

"Didn't you feel the earthquake this morning?" I asked,

"Yes, but that was a couple of hours ago," he replied.

"Well I was in the middle of it and had to wait for the fireman to use the ladder to get everyone out of the building I live in," I explained. "I will be there just as soon as I can," I said.

"Can you work till 6:30 PM tonight?" he asked.

'Not really. I have a standing date at that time," I said, keeping my fingers crossed hoping he would understand.

"With Jack?" he asked.

"Yes," I answered.

"Well that's an easy fix, just have him meet you here," he said almost laughing.

"Fine," I said. "See you in a little while," I added.

"You had better hurry. George will be coming by in eight minutes," Nell said urging me to speed up.

"Oh My! Where should I put this?" I asked holding up the bag.

"Put it in the spare bedroom," she said pointing down the hall.

I ran down the hallway and put the bag in one of the dresser drawers.

"You need to go NOW! she insisted.

"Thanks!" I yelled as I ran out the door.

I had just finished pulling my hair into a ponytail when George pulls up.

"Rita. You're at the wrong stop today.

What's up?" he asked as I got on.

"Didn't you feel the earthquake we had earlier this morning?" I asked while handing him my pass.

"No, I guess I was on the bumpy road while it was happening. What happened? Was it bad" he asked while I sat down right behind him.

"Well, I'll put it this way. I will be staying with Nell until housing is figured out," I said.

"Really, it was that bad?" he questioned.

"Our building is closed off for now. The firemen had to come and get everyone out of the building," I explained.

"Well at least you had Nell to help you," he said in a thankful tone.

"Yes, I am thankful for that. I tried to get out of going to work today. After all, a lot has happened since early this morning." I said with a chuckle. "But it didn't work, Charlie said, "Come in anyway," I added.

The rest of my ride to work was quiet and thought-provoking.

"Here you are," George announced.

"Thanks George, see you tomorrow if not sooner," I said getting off the bus.

Sandy caught me as soon as I open the door. "Rita! How bad was the quake where you live?" Sandy asked as I walked through the café door.

"Pretty rough," I answered as I looked around for Charlie, then back at Sandy.

"What about your place?" I asked putting on my apron.

"I'm not sure. I haven't been home yet and I live about twenty miles from here," She said with a smile.

"Well, hopefully, it will better than my place," I said spotting Charlie.

"Charlie, I really need to talk to you for a few," I said from across the room.

"Okay, after the rush is over. I'm glad you got here as soon as you did. I thought I was going to have to close for a while," He replied.

"Why what damage did the café get from the quake?" I asked looking around.

"Oh, nothing major. We have just gotten really busy and keep running out of things since all of that went down," he said quickly while stacking dishes.

"Yeah, business has been on overload since the quake. It seems that the Rooster is the only place nearby that still has electric and gas," Joy chimed in.

"Thanks for the update," I said smiling at both of them.

"Charlie, where do you need me the most?" I asked. It seemed that Sandy and Joy had the front of the café pretty much under control.

"BACK HERE!" I heard him yell from the back.

As I walked into the backroom I could see where he had a problem. The quake had pretty much scrambled the storage room.

"What a mess! Oh my goodness!" I said at seeing most of the shelves cleared and all the things that were on them on the floor. It looked like a very angry person had a fit in this room.

"If you think this room is bad, wait until you see the refrigerator. That is the area I need you in," he said looking up at me from the floor. "Do what you can as fast as you can. I need a list of what needs replacing so I can make a run to the warehouse on 3rd West." He added.

"Okay, I'm on it," I said grabbing the clipboard on my way to the refrigeration unit.

I didn't bother trying to pick anything up from the floor right off. I needed to make a list for him. So I looked around to see what was salvageable and what all needed to be replaced.

"Charlie here is the list I made from the walk-in frig," I said handing him the clipboard while reaching for the broom and a large box.

"I'm curious about something. Can we talk a little after I get this mess straightened out?" I asked.

"Sure when I get back from getting supplies," He said grabbing the clipboard.

While Charlie hurried off to the warehouse for supplies, I finished cleaning the refrigeration unit.

I walked out of the unit and looked at my watch. 'That didn't take as long as I thought. I still have a few minutes before the lunch rush gets going. I'm going to call Jack while I have a chance.' As I reached out for the phone, Charlie walked in pushing a hand cart stacked with supplies.

"Jimmy, Rita, there are more things to grab in the truck," he yelled while walking past us to the storeroom.

Jimmy was the first one to the back door. I grabbed a pushcart on my way out. I wasn't sure just how much was left.

After looking at the truck, it was a good thing I did. Most of the things that were left either went in the freezer or refrigerator. That would have meant very cold hands.

"Good thinking," Jimmy said looking around at me.

"My Mom always said, "Work hard but work smart," I said with a big grin.

"I want to get this done quick. I need to make a quick call and also talk to Charlie before the rush gets going strong." I informed Jimmy while putting things on the cart.

"It won't take long to get these things

put away," He said.

"Can you handle putting the things in the freezer then shovel the cart into the refer unit?" I asked. "That will give me a chance to call Jack real quick," I explained.

"Sure. Not a problem. The dished aren't stacking up that fast right now," He said laughing.

I had just remembered that I forgot to give Nell Jack's phone number.

"Thanks," I said rushing back to the phone.

"Hello?" Jack said.

"Hi Jack, It's me. Can you meet me at work instead of at my house today? Please. I will explain when I see you. I got called in," I said.

"Yes, I can do that." He answered. "Around 6 o'clock right," he added.

"Yes. Thanks. Bye," I said hanging up the phone just as Charlie rounded the corner.

"Did you get everything out of the truck?" he asked.

"Yes, but I still want to talk to you," I said.

"Is right here ok?" he asked.

"Yes, I was wondering if you noticed that Anna and I looked alike right away?" I asked.

Chapter Five

"No, I know you're kin now. No, she doesn't have freckles like you with her hair pulled back and she wears makeup and her hair was blonde and always fixed like she went to a beauty parlor and she wore really expensive clothes. So no, there were and are still a lot of differences between you and Anna. Why do you ask?" he stated.

"Oh. I was just wondering." I said with a smile

"Looks like I got back and things put where they belong just in time. The rush looks like it may be heavy today," he said looking towards the dining room. "Get out there and keep them happy." He added looking over at me.

"Ok," I said heading for the counter to grab my order pad and pen.

The people seem to come in to eat in bunches. Then when it got closer to dinner time it was back to a lot of couples.

Charlie had managed to have a special frame made for Anna's painting and had strategically placed lighting put into place that made the painting seem even more important. Then he had managed to get copies of a few of her other paintings and placed them in other places around the dining room. All of this seemed to draw in my couples in the evening.

The day moved along quickly.

Jack walked while I was in the back getting more plates.

"Rita, Jack just came in," Sandy said walking towards me and catching me halfway back to the front.

"Good," I said putting the dished into place. "Sally got here a few minutes ago and is ready to take my place," I added. "Charlie! I'm off," I yelled towards his office in the back. "Sally your up," I said looking over at here.

She had been having a coffee at a corner table.

"Hi Jack, did you want to eat here or go a couple of blocks over to Blakes Burger Barn?" I asked quietly after getting closer to him.

"Let's go to Blakes tonight. I heard there are a few shops nearby that may be interesting," He said.

I finished putting my apron in the hamper on the way out the door.

"See you tomorrow," I said as I walked through the door holding hands with Jack.

"What kind of shops have you heard about that's near Blakes Burger Barn?" I asked as Jack gave me a big smile.

"Oh I don't know. I've never been there," he said with a chuckle.

"You are being very mysterious this evening," I said walking a little faster.

"What's your hurry? We have plenty of time tonight," Jack said holding on to my hand trying to slow me down. "We have a few extra hours tonight," He added.

I slowed down and waited for him to catch up with me. "How did you get the few extra hours?" I questioned.

"Oh I did a few extra things for the boss this week and he added six hours to my twelve," he informed me.

"Can I ask what kind of things?" I asked hoping for an answer.

"Well. You can ask. But that doesn't mean you'll get an answer," he said laughing while we waited for the light to change.

"Oh that shop looks like one to visit," I said pointing to the one across the street.

"Ok. We can start there. You picked that one, so I get to pick the next one," He said giving a big smile.

"Ok deal," I said almost dragging him across the street when the light turned green.

I loved being with Jack. It was a lot of fun and we had great conversations. There never seemed to be a dull moment and I found myself enjoying life more than I had in a very long time.

It turned out that the shop I picked was one that carried most anything you would need if you were to go to the beach.

I love bright colors and found a brightly colored, flowered muumuu. I held it up with a big smile and said. "Look what I found,"

"Only if I get to wear this." He said holding up a shirt that at first glance you would think was poke a dotted but on second look it had flowers in the colored circles and then he matched in with a pair of large plaid Bermuda shorts.

"Oh My!" I exclaimed laughing while we put them back on the racks.

Then we found face masks with the snorkel tubes. We both grabbed one and put it up to our faces. We looked at each other and both started laughing again as we put them back.

Then I found the swimsuits. I hadn't been to the beach in so long and the last time I went I didn't have a swimsuit so I waded in my shorts and an old tee shirt.

I found a brightly colored one-piece and I held it up and looked over at Jack who had found the watches.

He looked up and saw the swimsuit. "Go try it on. I want to see it on you," he said.

As I walked out of the dressing room to where the multi mirrors were, he caught sight of me and gave a soft whistle.

I gave him a smile hoping I wasn't turning as red as I felt I was.

He gently tossed me a floppy brimmed straw hat from the shelf near him. As I put it on one of the clerks walked up behind him.

"She is quite pretty. Isn't she?" she asked him.

He said "Yes." as he turned to see who was talking. "That's MY girl," he said with a large smile, then turned and gave me a wink.

Hearing the words, 'my girl', made me feel really good. It let me know how he felt about me. I couldn't hold back the big smile that was forcing its way out.

I took those few steps that were between us and gave him a hug and took a quick kiss. Then I turned and ran to the dressing room and changed back into my clothes.

We walked out of the store smiling

and I was carrying a sack with the hat and swimsuit I had just tried on.

"Now remember the next store in my choice," he said with a soft chuckle.

"Ok, where to next," I asked while we stood on the sidewalk and he looked up and down the street.

"That one!" he said pointing to a large store in the middle of the next block.

When we got closer I could see that it was one of the larger department stores in our area.

I hadn't been to this store. I never felt I had the money and didn't want to temp myself. After all, if you don't know what you are missing then it doesn't cross your mind to want it.

"Come on, this will be fun," Jack coaxed taking me by the hand and almost pulling me into the store.

As we walked in, I almost became aw struck. The store seemed larger inside than it looked from the outside.

There were so many things to look at and isles leading in all different directions.

Then I noticed that Jack was still holding my hand. "Let's go this way first," he said with a gentle tug.

I looked back in the direction he was leading me and seen a jewelry counter. There was a man standing behind the counter and as we got closer Jack held up my hand and pointed to my finger. I thought I was going to lose my breath. I felt flush and held tight to Jack's hand. Everything went black for a moment then it was all ok again just as fast.

We sat down at a lower counter and the man pulled out a tray of rings.

"Which one do you like?" Jack asked.

I felt stunned for a moment and looked at him. I guess I looked a little surprised and confused at the same time.

He laughed and said. "This is the cheaper version I want you to have until I can get to San Francisco to get you a better one. That is if you want me to follow you there?" he questioned.

"I do I really do want you to come there. Thinking about leaving you here was making me feel sad,." I said giving him a big hug.

"So this is like a promise ring. A promise of something bigger to last longer in the future," He said grabbing both my hand as he leaned over and gave me a quick kiss.

"I like that one with the heart and the small diamond in the center of the heart," I said pointing to the smaller case.

The man reached back into the case and brought out the tray holding the pretest ring I had ever seen. "This one?" he asked, taking it out and handing it to Jack.

"Yes," I said. "That is so pretty," I added.

"Then we will take this on and a gold necklace to hold it," Jack said handing the ring back to the man.

"Very nice choice," The man said as he got up to get a tray of gold necklaces before sitting down again.

"Which one of the necklaces would you like for this ring to be placed on?" he asked looking at both of us.

"How about this one?" Jack asked looking at me.

I was so busy smiling to really answer. So I just nodded.

"Good choice. Shall I wrap it?" the man asked.

"No, I don't think that is necessary," Jack said looking at me.

I held my ponytail up while Jack fastened it around my neck. "Then this makes it official. You are my girlfriend." Jack said giving me a big kiss.

I could feel myself turning red as I looked around to see if anyone saw that kiss. "Are we going steady then?" I asked just to clarify.

"Yes, that is why it is called a promise

ring. We only see each other and no others,"
He added.

"I agree and that is just fine with me,"
I said.

Jack paid for the ring and necklace,
and then reached for my hand. I had a deep
smile as we walked away from the counter
holding hands.

"Are you happy Rita?" Jack asked
sending love with his eyes.

"Yes, more than ever before," I
answered as we both leaned in for a kiss.

"I know I never really asked formally
but will you be my girl?" he asked while
putting his arm around me as we sat down
on a bench just outside the store.

Yes! Oh Yes!" I said clutching the ring
that now hung around my neck.

"So what all have you done to get
ready for the move to San Francisco?" he
asked.

"Well I have been reading about it,
and I have made a few calls to a few
companies there about places to live. I
wanted to get some idea about the prices of
things. I ordered a phonebook so I can look
up places that maybe I can get a job with," I
said.

"Good. I'm not sure yet but I may be
able to help a little." Jack said with a smile.

"How?" I asked

"I'm not real sure yet but I may have a
few ideas. I just haven't figured out how to
work them into the equations yet," He said

smiling at me. "But right now, let's go eat. My stomach is letting me know its empty," he added with a chuckle.

"Oh Yes! Let's. I do feel it now that you mentioned it. I guess I was too excited to feel it before," I said giving out a slight giggle.

We held hands and talked all the way to the burger barn and it all seemed so natural to me as if it was to be this way.

We decided during our meal that we had time to go see the movie that was playing nearby. It was a double feature and we found ourselves making out during the second feature.

"That first movie was pretty interesting but I think I liked the second one the best," Jack said softly as we walked out of the theater.

With that, I had to giggle.

"It's getting late and I need to get back to work. I have enough time to walk you home and catch the bus," he said while reaching out for my hand.

"It's nice walking and holding hands with the one you love. Not a word needs to be said." I thought as we walked along just enjoying each other's company.

As we walked past where I used to live, we both paused for a moment.

"Wow, I am glad you didn't get hurt in all of that. What a mess," Jack said giving me a squeeze.

Jack walked me up to Nell's place and

we got in a few more kisses. "You had better get going. The bus will be coming by in a few minutes," I prompted.

"Oh! It is later than I thought," he said looking at his watch. "Bye, love you," he added as he almost ran down the few steps.

"As I turned to grab the doorknob, Nell opened it and Anna was standing right besides her looking at me. "Meow, Meow." She said.

"Yes I know I was gone a little longer than you thought I should have been. But a lot happened today." I said as I walked in and tossing my jacket over the back of the couch and sitting down.

Anna bounced onto the couch beside me and sat there looking at me while Nell sat down across from me in her favorite chair.

"What a day! Oh my gosh, where to start." I said while petting Anna.

"How about from this morning?" Nell said while leaning forward raising one eyebrow and giving a big smile.

Chapter Six

"Ok. Well, I went to work as you know. And Boy! What a mess. Jack walked into the café just as I got off work and we walked over to the shops near Smith Street.

I got a new swimsuit and hat.' I said while pulling it off.

"Yes, I noticed the hat as you walked into the house. Nell said with a slight giggle. "It's cute and you look good in it. I hadn't thought of you as a hat person. So what else did you do?" she prodded with a large smile.

"We had a lot of fun. He told one of the clerks that I was his girl." I said with an ear to ear smile.

"And..?" Nell questioned.

"He picked out the next store and this is what he got me," I said with a giggle as I reached for and pulled the chain into view with the ring hanging from it.

"A ring!" Nell almost shouted. "So are you going steady now?" she questioned.

"Yes, he asked me to be his girl, officially, after giving me the ring," I explained.

"Wow, that is so great," Nell said excitedly. "I am glad for you. But there are so many questions that all of this brings up," she continued.

"Like what?" I asked, while still playing with the ring.

"Well how are you doing on finding a place to rent in San Francisco?" she asked.

"Well I have called a few places and things are real pricy out there. But I do have a lead on a studio. The owner and I have been talking on the phone and she has one that is to open up in the next few months," I said.

"So what about Jack at that point? Long distant relationships have problems most of the time," she warned.

"I know, but Jack said he thinks he has a few ideas about my move. I didn't ask him much about it. After all, he has a special job here and I don't think I will be there but a few months at the most," I explained.

"Well you know what you need to do and I know that Jack has been helping a lot here and there in all of this," she said with a chuckle.

"Meow," Anna said as she stood up, stretched and then trotted off to the kitchen.

"I think she is trying to tell me something," I said laughing.

She got to the kitchen door, turned and meowed again very loudly.

"Oh, getting pushy are w? I said

laughing. "I'm on my way," I said getting up to follow her.

Nell followed me. "It is about time to have something to eat. Are you hungry Rita?" she asked.

"Meow," Anna said.

"Yes. I know you are hungry for more than you dry food that is still in your bowl," Nell said with a chuckle after looking toward her bowl. "I put her can food on the shelf under the sink. And the can opener is in the drawer next to the sink," she added.

"Jack and I ate a big meal at Blake's Burger Barn," I said while feeding Anna.

"Oh well, then you won't have to eat for a week," she said laughing. "They have the largest burgers I have ever seen and they pile the fries so high. Did you get their shake too?" she asked with a giggle.

"Well of course," I said adding to the laughter.

I sat at the table and drank a soda while chatting with Nell while she ate her dinner. Then we watched a little TV and headed off to bed.

I slept till my alarm went off and still felt a little sleeping as I followed Anna to the kitchen.

"Good morning Rita and Anna," Nell said with a big smile as we walked it. "How did you two sleep?"

"God, but it is a good thing I had the alarm set," I said.

"Why is that?" she asked.

"Because your bed is really comfy and there is no bright sun shining through the window to wake me up," I said laughing. "Anna even wanted to sleep in this morning," I added.

"Well breakfast is ready. I hope eggs and cereal is ok this morning. I forgot to ask what you like last night before we went to sleep," she added.

"All of this is great. Oh! And Anna didn't even have to ask. She is going to get so spoiled," I said with a chuckle.

"Nell, while you are at work today, do you think you can find out what the procedure is for getting temp housing after a quake like we just had. I don't know if the building I lived in had insurance that will help with that of not. I don't even know what needs to be done next?" I asked.

"I am sure someone in my office will know something about what needs to be done next," she said. "But you know you are welcome to stay here till you leave for San Francisco. I mean it's not like you can afford to take furniture with you. I mean it will be cheaper to get what you need once you get there. A studio isn't all that big. If you stay here then you can sell what you don't need and save the money to help make the move easier," she explained.

"True. But are you sure?" I asked. "But I still think it would be a good idea to see what they say," I said.

"You know I just got to thinking. It's a

good thing we are the same size. We have about half an hour before George comes by. Follow me," Nell said motioning for me to follow.

We walked into her bedroom.

"I figure it will be at least four days before the safety groups say it's safe for anyone to go back into your apartment building. Take these and put them in your room so you will have clothes to wear till them," she said handing me a bundle of clothes she had laying on the bed.

"Are you sure? Because I could work in these today and buy a few things after work today," I questioned.

"Sure what is family for if not to help when needed," she said laughing. "After all we are pretty much like sisters. We've been in each other's lives for a very long time," she added and I joined her in the laughter.

"Ok," I said taking the close and hurriedly getting dressed.

As I came out of the bedroom with Anna on my heels, Nell met me in the hall

"We have to hurry. George will be coming by in about seven minutes," she said.

"Anna you be a good girl. Nell has a very nice place for you to sit in the window and watch the traffic." I told her while petting her and placing her by the window.

"We can leave the TV on, if you want. That way she won't leave alone," Nell offered.

"Thanks," I said as I turned it on just

as Nell opened the front door. "Now Anna, you be a good girl and I will be back after work," I said as I closed the door.

"Hurry, here come George!" Nell shouted from the sidewalk. "Run. Let's see if we can get there before him. He has one stop before he gets to us," she said as we both gain speed.

"Hi George," we both said almost in unison between pants.

"You two are getting good at running," he said trying not to laugh.

We paid our fares and made our way back to the seat we usually sat in. The ride seemed shorter today.

"Ok see you after work," I said giving Nell a short wave.

"Bye George, see you after work," I yelled as I got off the bus.

'It feels strange going to work in Nell's clothes. But there was no way of getting out of it. Maybe I can get hold of Jerry on my break and talk him into going back into my apartment and emptying my draws and clothes into a bag for me,' I thought.

"Good morning Sandy," I said as I walked through the door. She was standing at the register taking care of a customer.

"Oh hi Rita," she said glancing at me.

I went straight to the back and put on the larges apron I could find. I didn't want anything to happen to Nell's clothes.

The Rooster stayed very busy until about thirty minutes before the lunch run usually started.

'Betty should be here most any minute now and then I can go make the call to Jerry,' I thought looking at my watch. 'Good, there she is, right on time.'

As Betty came walking from the backroom of the café tying the strings of her apron I managed to catch her as she reached the counter.

"I need to make a quick phone call. I will be quick. They lunch crowd is just beginning," I said rushing past her.

The phone rang four times at the firehouse. 'Come on someone has to be there,' I thought as it rang again. "Come on Jerry pick up," I said as I started to pace.

"Hello Central Station, Jerry speaking," Came the voice over the phone.

"Oh good Jerry, just the person I needed to talk to. I need your help," I said.

"Rita? Is that you?" he asked.

"Oh yes sorry. Is there a way you can go by my apartment and get my clothes from my drawers and at least a few shirts from the closet?" I asked quickly.

"I'm not sure I will ask the chief when he gets back. Are you at Nell's?" he asked.

"Yes, but at work right now" I answered.

"Good, then I will let you know as soon as I find out," he answered quickly then hung up.

I hurried back to the front of the café just in time as a group of eight walked in.

Betty gave me a nod to take care of them.

With the help of one of the young men we pulled two tables together and gathered the chairs for all of them.

The day went fast and the tips were great. I had just put my apron away when George walked in for his coffee.

"Hi George, are you on time or a little ahead today?" I asked handing him a cup to go of hot coffee.

"Real close, but I figure I have about five sips of coffee before getting on the bus again," he said with a chuckle between sips." Why you ready to go already?" he asked smiling.

"Yes, I feel a little uneasy about leaving Anna alone at Nell's all day," I said standing at the door.

"Oh that's right. I had forgotten about the quake and you staying at Nell's now," he said being a little more serious. "Ok, let's go," he said pushing the door the rest of the way open.

I put my coins in the meter and made my way back to where Nell was sitting.

"Hi. Where you able to get any information about how the insurance works with the owner of my old apartment?" I asked.

"Not really. I asked around and no one seemed to know how all of that works. I will try to call a few of the insurance companies tomorrow," she said. "It will work out the way it is supposed to. How did your day go?" she added.

"Pretty good, we did good on tips today. And Jerry is going to ask if he can go back into my apartment and get my clothes. When we get home, uh, back to your place. I would like to check my emails. I sent off a few emails asking questions to different places, about renting in San Francisco," I said.

"Of course, you can do that while I make us dinner," she said with a big smile. "Our stop is next," she said nudging me to stand up.

"Bye George," we said together as we got off the bus.

Anna met us at the door. "Meow," then ran to the kitchen as she meowed the second time. We both had to laugh because of the comical sounded she was making.

"Ok baby girl. I see you have made yourself at home," as I walked through the kitchen door. She was sitting very royal like next to her dish waiting to be served.

"I do have to say she is very well minded," Nell said going to the refrigerator and handing me the milk.

"Only when she wants to be, she can be pretty demanding when she wants," I said laughing as I poured the milk into her bowl. I will get you some more food in a little while. Meanwhile drink this slowly," I instructed her while petting her.

"I'm going to check my emails and see if anyone got back to me," I informed Nell.

"Yes of course. I will get started on dinner. It should take about half an hour. Will that be enough time?" she questioned.

"I think so. I didn't write that many people," I said.

It wasn't long before Anna came trotting into the living room as if she was proud of something and jumped upon the desk. I quickly leaned over the computer keyboard to keep her from stepping or lying down on it.

"Anna, you need to go lay on the couch for a few minutes and let me finish what I am trying to do," I scolded.

She jumped down letting out a "Meow" like a spoiled child talking back.

"I love you and you know that. But I really need to get this done," I explained.

She laid down on the couch, tucking her front paws under her chest while letting out a soft "Mow" then closed one eye.

I looked back at the screen and my eyes caught one email that stood out among all of the others. "APT in S.F." was written in the subject heading.

I quickly clicked on it. My heart was picking up speed with anticipation and I caught myself holding my breath. Just then the lights blinked and the computer went off.

"Oh Man!" I caught myself saying out loud in almost a shout.

Chapter Seven

Nell came running from the kitchen to the living room. "Are you ok?" she asked.

"Yes, the computer shut down when the lights blinked and I had just clicked to open the email that looked real interesting," I explained.

"Ok," she said sounding relieved. "That was what I call a brownout. The electric hic-ups and some things shut down, like the computer, it's pretty sensitive to fluctuations in power. Just turn it back on. Everything will still be where it was, but you will need to load the page you were on. I work with computers every day and so I try to stay off of it when I get home," she explained.

"Oh good," I said in relief.

"Dinner is ready anyway. You can try again after we eat," she said walking back toward the kitchen with Anna following.

Anna sat in the corner next to her plate and meowed. "Anna, you will get to eat but you will need to wait for a little while. The rules here are a little different than it was at our house," I said.

"I will make sure she has plenty to eat before I leave the kitchen," Nell said.

"She is a spoiled baby. Aren't you Anna?" I said looking at her. "You sit right there and you will get to eat in a little while," I explained.

"That was a great dinner. Thank you, Nell," I said while carrying my plate to the sink.

"If you don't mind I will give Anna the leftovers," she offered. "I don't like leftovers," she added.

"I don't mind and I'm sure she won't mind," I said with a chuckle as Anna stood on her back legs and front paws together as if to beg.

Nell filled Anna's plate and placed it on the floor. The way she started eating, you would think she hadn't eaten in a very long time.

I stayed in the kitchen and help where ever I could. When everything was clean, dried and put away we both headed for the living room.

Nell and I made out way to the living room she turned on the TV.

"I always watch the news this time of evening," she said

I motioned towards the computer. "Oh sure, go ahead," she added.

Anna came into the room almost prancing with her head and tail held high in the air, jumped up onto the couch and laid down as if she owned it.

"You are a funny cat Anna," Nell said as she reached out and petted her.

After a few minutes, I got the email open that I saw earlier.

The email read.
"Hello, Rita,

I got your inquiry about the apartment ad that I had posted online.

The apartment will be available as of the 15th of April.

I will allow your one cat because it is considered a companion pet.

The deposit of $300 needs to be in my hands by the first of April for me to hold it for you.

The apartment is a studio on the 2nd floor and it includes a 5ftx 5ft storage area in the basement. The rent is $375 per month and there is no lease.

I am willing to prorate the rent so that it falls due on the 1st of each month.

Email me as to your plans. I will eccept Postal M.O. or Certified bank check.

Sincerely yours
Beca March

228 Lauren St
San Francisco, CA
94118

Questions (415)628-7808

––––––––––––––––––––––––––––––––––––––

"Nell? Can I use your printer and print out this email?" I asked excitedly.

"Sure. So you think this is the one you are going to take?" she asked from the couch.

"I think so. It sounds small but I can always move if I find one better later. Anna and I will need to travel there by bus, and I found out that will take us a couple of days. But that fits in with the money I have saved, so far" I explained.

"Do you have enough saved for a few months rent just in case you don't find work right away?" Nell questioned.

"Yes, I have enough for four months in savings. And I still have a month and a half before I have to send Beca the check." I said feeling so excited I could hardly contain myself. "I will need to get a pet carrier so Anna can ride the bus with me," I added.

I looked at my watch. "Good, it's not too late. Is it alright if I use your phone to call Jack?" I asked.

"Go for it. I'm sure he will want to know what you have planned and that you found a place to live in San Fran," Nell said while turning the TV volume back up.

"Thanks," I said going to the bedroom to make the call.

It didn't take long before Anna can in and jumped onto the bed next to where I was sitting.

"Hello, Jack?" I said as the phone was lifted on the other end.

"Hi Rita," he said. "I recognized your voice. What is going on?"

"I got an email back from a person

with an apartment for rent in San Francisco today. Is there a way you can find out where Anna uh my art teacher is going to be in San Francisco," I ask.

"You know I may have that written down somewhere. I got to wondering about different things after getting to know you better and I asked for a little more information that may be needed later. Hold on for a minute and I will get my notebook," he said laying the phone down.

I could hear him shuffling papers then he came back to the phone.

"I didn't write down the address but I do have the street name. He will have an art shop on Clay Street. I would like to meet you again this Wednesday after work like we did this last. I have a small tracker I want to put in your ring. That way I will always know you are ok. Also if you lose it or something we can find it," he said.

"Ok. I know I won't lose it because I only take it off while I'm in the shower. Because I don't want to take a chance of it falling off and going down the drain," I said.

"That's ok. But trust me there are other reasons that I am not allowed to talk to you about. Nothing to worry about, it will make it easier to find you later on. Because I want to be able to come see you when my boss finally lets me have a real vacation. " he said with a chuckle. "I love you. Duty is calling, have to go to work," he added.

"Love you too," I said just as he hung

up.

I have not more than hung the phone up when it rang.

"Hello?" I said.

"Rita, is that you?" the voice said.

"Yes," I answered.

"This is Jerry," he said.

"Oh Hi Jerry. I didn't recognize your voice. You sound different tonight. What's up," I asked.

"The Chief said I could go get your things tomorrow while we are clearing and sealing up your old apartment building," he informed me.

"Oh thank you. I should be home by six pm. Can you bring my things to Nell's house after that?" I questioned.

"Yes, I'm sure I can do that. It will be on my way home," he said. "bye," he said and the phone went to dial tone.

I hung you and went back to the living room.

Nell was just getting up to turn the TV off.

"Who called?" she asked.

"Oh that was Jerry saying that he can bring by things from my apartment tomorrow after six," I told her.

"Oh good we will be home by then," she said.

"That's what I figured," I agreed.

"Time for bed, morning will come fast enough," she added.

"True, Anna is already laying down," I

said laughing. "Good Night Nell," I said heading for the guest bedroom.

"Good girl," I told Anna while getting ready for bed.

She lifted her head and gave a soft meow and laid down again.

"Good night baby," I said as I crawled into bed and closed my eyes.

I tossed and turned all night. I dreamed that the room was only large enough for a twin bed and so small that you only had room enough to stand at the side of the bed and cook and the bathroom door just had room enough to open part way and there was one very small closed that had a single door that slid back into the way to be opened.

My alarm went off just as I really fell asleep.

I got up and got dressed in another set of Nell's clothes. As I left the bedroom and headed down the hall to the kitchen Anna was on my heels.

"Good Morning," Nell said cheerfully.

"Oh, good morning," I said as Anna meowed her good morning.

I grabbed a cup out of the cabinet, filled it with coffee and sat down at the table. I soon found myself sitting there half asleep with my head held up by both hands.

"Trouble sleeping?" Nell asked.

"Yeah sort of a night mare," I said.

"About what? Care to share?" Nell prodded.

"I think maybe I should have asked how large the studio is in my last email. I dreamed it was even too small to walk in. I would have to crawl over the twin bed to get from the sink and stove to the bathroom," I explained.

"Now that is what I would call small," Nell said with a chuckle. "You know it wouldn't hurt to call and ask how large the room is," she suggested.

"True I can do that when I get back this evening," I said with a breath of relief.

"Meanwhile, breakfast is ready," Nell said putting two bowls of oatmeal on the table and a plate with toast. Then she went to the refrigerator and got another plate of food for Anna. She placed it on the floor then joined me at the table.

"It's a good day and I am sure that the room will be larger than the one in your dream. Don't worry about it. If it isn't large enough then it isn't the place you are supposed to be and another place will show up when the time is right for you to move," Nell advised.

"Very true. Thank you for taking us in and making meals for us," I said with a smile and we could hear Anna purring loudly her thank you which caused both of us to giggle.

"Oh my! It is a little later than I thought," Nell said excitedly. "George will be by in about fifteen min and I have to do my makeup yet. Can you rinse the dishes this morning?" Nell asked running for the bathroom.

"Yes, not a problem," I answered quickly. "Lucky I don't wear makeup. Huh Anna?" I said quietly. While rinsing off all the dished and silverware used that morning.

"I heard that," Nell said laughing.

"Well?" I said joining the laughter.

I had just filled Anna's bowls with water and dry food when Nell came back into the kitchen.

"Ready?" she asked, tuning towards the door. "Come on," she added motioning for me to hurry.

I ran out the front door and Nell closed it behind us and we raced to the bus stop, laughing the whole way.

"Yeah we won!" I shouted as George pulled up and opened the doors of the bus.

"Not by much!" he exclaimed laughing.

"Maybe not by much but we did it," I said and we all laughed even more.

Some of the others regulars on the bus, ride at the same time as us, joined in the laughter.

After all, riding the same bus at the same time nearly every day, people get to know each other and feel safe sharing things like laughter.

We made our way back to our favorite seats and sat down.

"I will try to get time to ask what compensation is usually given to people who are displaced because of natural damages, like earthquakes," Nell informed me.

"Oh good. Thank you. Here's my stop. I'll see you later," I said heading for the door.

"Later George," I said giving him a wave, as I got off the bus.

"Morning Joy," I said as I walked into The Roster.

"Oh, hi Rita. Charlie said he wanted to see you as soon as you got here," she reported.

"Ok, thanks" I said heading past her towards the back room. I grabbed my apron and headed for Charlie's office.

"You wanted to see me?" I asked.

"yeah. I heard you were learning how to paint," he said still thumbing through a few things on his desk.

"Yes, but nothing close to what Anna has done. Why?" I asked.

"Do you have any pictures of them, so I can see what kind of pictures you are painting?" he asked.

"Not with me. But I can get some made and bring them in on another day, if you want me to," I said.

"Yes. Please do that. If you are half as good as your sister I may want to buy a few for the back way," he said with a smile, then looked at his watch. "To work with you," he said shooing me with his hands.

I pulled my hair up into a bun with a smile as I made my way to the front counter.

"Sammy called to reserve four tables

for six o'clock today. It seems it is his nephew's ninth birthday," Joy informed me.

"Is there a special setup he wants or just the tables reserved?" I asked.

"He is dropping off the balloons and crape ribbons on his lunch break," she shouted from the back.

"Good," I said as she came back to the front.

Morning went fast. Most of our customers between breakfast rush and noon are seniors that come in to rest after doing their walks.

I just finished clearing and cleaning the first table to be used for Sammy's party as he walked in.

"Hello Sammy. Are these all of the balloons you want set up for the party," I asked taking them from him.

"Yes but I have to go get the rest of the stuff from my car," he said turning to go out the door.

"Joy? Did Sammy mention how many people he thought was coming?" I asked while he was outside.

"No, that may be a good thing to find out," she said laughing.

"You Think?" I said joining her while tying the balloons to one of the chairs.

Charlie came out of his office just as Sammy came back in carrying two good size boxes.

"Hi Sammy, I see the boxes what are we doing for you this time?" Charlie

questioned.

"It's all for my nephew's ninth birthday party. I'm supplying the cake and you still have ice cream right?" Sammy asked.

"Yes, but for how many people are we talking about?" Charlie asked looking at me and Joy with a smile. We both shrugged our shoulders at him.

Sammy put the boxes on one of the back tables and stood there for what seemed like minutes stroking his chin. "Well I figure if everyone shows up, there should be about fifteen. No make that sixteen countings me," he said laughing. "I called you last week about this Charlie," he added with a big grin.

"Oh?" Charlie said.

"Yeah, it was Monday morning and I said I would need a few tables and we made a deal for use of the space. Plus whatever food that they order," he said.

"Oh yeah, now I remember. Sorry, it's been a crazy few days already," Charlie apologized.

"Oh, that's ok. Blame it on the years," Sammy said laughing.

"Hey now, we aren't that old yet I hope," Charlie said joining in.

They both sat down and joy went back to the front to take care of some of the customers we had and I went after two coffees for Charlie and Sammy.

As if I went back to the front Joy caught me by the arm." I hope Charlie lets us know how many tables we need to set up…soon. With two boxes of things to put up and the rest of the decorations, it may take us a little while," she said sounding a little worried.

"Oh, not to worry. I'm sure between the two of us we can get it done even if we have to decorate half of the café," I assured her with a smile.

Chapter Eight

I waved at Sammy as he walked out the door and managed to catch Charlie as he walked past.

"How many tables do you want set up?" I asked. Looking over and giving Joy a wink.

"I think we can set up four of the longer tables and that should be enough." He said as he passed me. "But do a good job." He added with a big grin.

"Always Charlie," I said with a chuckle.

"Betty should be here in about two hours and then we can start decorating for the party," I said.

"Oh that is right. Good, for some reason I had forgotten she was working today," Joy said letting out a long breath of relief, then a large smile.

"Feel better now?" I questioned with a small giggle.

"Yes, thanks for the reminder," she said while stacking the clean plates that

Jimmy had just brought to the front.

Time seemed to fly as we started to get things set for the dinner crowd.

"Betty!" Good, I'm glad you're here early," I said giving her a large smile.

"Why is that?" she asked. "I see something is up since you gave me your largest cheesy grin," she laughed.

"Oh Sammy came in earlier and we have to set up for his party and we only have about an hour and a half," I explained.

"Then you had better get started," she said heading for the back for her apron.

"We had better see what all he has in these boxes he left with us," I said motioning for Joy to follow me.

"Oh My goodness, are you seeing all of this?" she asked.

"Yes, and I am hoping that he isn't expecting all of it to be put up," I said looking over at her with a straight face.

"There are a lot of rolls of streamers in different colors, ribbons, signs, and banners. Oh good, there is a roll of tape," she said as she rummaged around in the box.

"Well this one has all of the hats, noisemakers, games, and party favors. Oh, and there are special plates, cups, and napkins," I informed her.

"Oh! I just found the table covers he wants used. They were at the bottom of the box." She announced.

"You know I think we should just empty the boxes on one of the tables and then start setting up. That way we will know everything we have to work with," I suggested.

"Excellent idea," she said dumping out the first box onto the table.

I followed suit with the second box.

Before long we had the tables pushed together and covered. We had just enough balloons to have one tied to each chair. There were so many streamers that one would think they were in streamer heaven. It took us longer to get the streamers set up than anything else. I held the ladder for Joy and then she held it for me. The tape didn't want to hold the streamers up we had to use all of the thumbtacks we could find.

Charlie came out to pass on his approval just as we finished and was carrying the empty box to the back.

I caught sight of the clock on the way through the kitchen. "Oh my, today went fast. It is almost time for George to be here," I caught myself saying aloud.

"Then you had better hurry!" Jimmy shouted over the spraying sound of the dishwasher.

Joy had already grabbed her purse and left by the time I got my jacket and got back to the front

Judy was walking through the doors just in front of George. She was the new waitress Charlie had just hired a few weeks back for the evening shift.

"Hi, Judy, Joy and I got everything set

up for Sammy's party. So it is all yours and Betty's from here," I said with a big smile.

"Hi George, are you on time of running fast?" I asked with a chuckle.

"I have a short time for a small coffee," he chuckled.

I handed him half a cup of coffee and I took the same amount of soda. We finished our drinks and I raced him to the bus. We both got on laughing.

I paid my fare and made my way back to Nell and the seat she always saved for me

"How did your day go?" Nell asked as I sat down.

"Good, pretty steady all day. Sammy, one of Charlie's friends came by and had us set up part of the café for a party later this evening. We had just finished decorating as George walked in," I informed her with a smile. "What happened to you today?" I asked

"Same O Same O. Oh but I did hear back from my insurance friend about the building you lived in," she said with a big grin.

"So, what did he say?" I asked.

"He said based on the size of your apartment, you should be getting a check for the amount of two months' rent to help replace anything that had to be left behind. Like bedroom sets, couch, TV, and kitchen table set," she said.

"Ok, I guess that would be about right," I agreed.

"That is unless you could prove with receipts that your things were bought new in the last year," she said laughing.

"No, most of what I had was hand me downs or second hand," I said joining the laughter.

"Well here comes our stop," she said leading the way to the back door of the bus. "See you in the morning George!" I shouted with a wave as we got off.

After dinner was over and the kitchen was clean we all (Me, Anna, and Nell) went to the living room to watch TV.

We had just got settled when the doorbell rang.

"Oh that must be Jerry," I said getting up to answer the door.

I opened the door to be surprised. "Oh. Hi Mat. I was expecting Jerry to come by tonight," I said while opening the door.

"Hi Rita, I know Jerry was to bring these to you tonight," he said handing me the large garbage bag through the door. "He went in with permission from our chief, to gather your things but fell as his foot went through the floor and he broke his arm. But he wanted you to have these tonight, so I brought them over instead," he said.

"Well thank you. Is Jerry ok? I mean how bad is the break?" I asked.

"Oh not bad. It is just a crack in his forearm. His wrist and elbow aren't involved and so that is good," he informed me as he stepped away from the door.

"Oh, that is good. Well tell Jerry I said thanks a lot and to mend fast," I said giving Mat a wave goodbye.

"Who was it, Rita?" Nell yelled.

"Oh it was Mat. He brought over my clothes and things from my dresser," I said on my way down the hall to the bedroom.

"Jerry fell and broke his arm today," I said as I got closer to the living room. "But he is ok," I said while sitting.

"Oh, I almost forgot. Charlie wants to see pictures of my painting. Can you take pictures of a few?" I asked.

"Yes, I am sure we can manage to get that done. But it will have to be tomorrow night. I will get more film tomorrow," she said.

We watched a few more programs and then called it a night.

Morning found me all snuggled in with my blanket tucked around my ears. But as soon as I moved the smallest amount Anna was up and giving a big yawn and long stretch. Then off she ran towards the kitchen meowing as she went as if to say "Come on, it's food time."

I stretched and got out of bed, got dressed in my own clothes and started down the hall towards the kitchen.

"Good morning," Nell said as she came out of her room. "Night seemed to go fast. At least for me," she said.

"Yeah, it seemed that way for me too. We didn't stay up that late did we?" I

questioned.

"No, not really. Guess we were more tired than we thought," she said.

"Oh My!" we both said in almost unison as we entered the kitchen, looked at the clock and realized we only had a half an hour before George came by.

"Looks like cold cereal this morning, right?" she said.

"Yep, sounds about right," I said while getting Anna fed and things set up for her day.

Nell had already sat down to eat. I knew I could take a little longer eating than she could because she hadn't put on her makeup yet.

She came back from her room and asked if I was ready to go just as I had finished washing our dishes.

"Yes and I think we may have to run a little," I said laughing.

"I agree," she said as we hurried down the steps to the sidewalk.

"Run!" I said "I see the bus and we still had about one hundred feet to go," I added.

"It's hard to run and laugh at the same time but we managed to get to the bus stop just as George opened the doors.

"You two are so funny. I look forward to this race nearly every day," he laughed while we caught our breath between giggles.

We hurriedly got to our seats as George stepped on the gas.

"I think George may be running a little late today," I whispered to Nell.

"I think your right. Things are flying by pretty fast this morning," she whispered trying no to laugh out loud.

Then we both did that quiet giggle when you think something is funny, but don't want to explain anyone as to what it is you're laughing about.

"Here comes my stop. See you later at home," I said. "I'm meeting Jack again at work when I get off. Remember the film," I added.

"Later George!" I yelled as I got off the bus.

I was hoping for a slow day that would go by quickly. Thinking that way I would have plenty of energy for when Jack came by to meet me.

"Hi Rita," Charlie said just as I opened the door.

"Hi, what's up," I asked. Charlie doesn't say Hi like that unless there is something that he needs done right away.

"We got in all of our shipments today, pretty much back to back and Jimmy needs help organizing things and getting them put away. And since you are good at that, you are in charge," he explained pointing towards the back.

"Ok, on my way," I said going for my apron.

"Hi Jimmy. Charlie gave me the impression that everything came in about the same time," I said as I met him near the back door.

"Well look for yourself," he said pointing the delivery dock.

"I my gosh. I guess so. Well, we had better get started or we will be here for a very long time," I said. "Do you have the checklist?" I asked.

"Yeah, right here," he said handing me a clipboard with about four pages on it.

We worked all morning and finally brought in the last box about twelve ten.

Jimmy and I took a peek into the kitchen while taking the last box into the freezer. The dished were stacked high in several rows next to the sink.

"Oh my, dang-it anyway. I leave the kitchen for a few hours and it looks like an army came through," he said slightly under his breath. But I heard him.

"I will help Jimmy and it would take that long to get things under control again," I said trying to let him know he wasn't alone. I had his back.

"Ok, I'm going to take you up on that," he said with a chuckle.

It only took us a little over an hour and the kitchen dishes were back to normal. Then the rest of my day was getting the boxes unpacked, inspecting everything and putting it all in the right places on the right shelves.

I managed to grab a bite here and there while working to get it all settled. I didn't mind working like that because I could take my time for the most part.

It wasn't long before I heard Charlie yell from the front. "Rita, Jack's here. Are you done back there?" he asked.

"Yes. I will be there is a few minutes," I said. I had to put away my apron yet and grab my jacket.

"Hi Jack," I said reaching for his hand.

He reached over and gave me a quick kiss. "Are you off work?" he asked.

"Yes, and ready to go," I said. "Bye everyone, see you later," I announced as we walked out the door.

"We need to go back to my place today," he said.

"Ok," I said as we walked to the bus stop.

"Hi George," I said as we got on the bus.

"Hi Rita. Where are you two headed?" George asked.

"We are going to the 2300 block of States street," Jack spoke up.

"Oh then here, you will need these. I can let you know when your stop comes up," George said handing Jack the transfers.

"Ok, thanks," Jack said taking them.

We sat down right behind George so we could hear him when our stop came.

Jack put his arm around me and we sat and listened to the people on the bus. It seemed extra loud today. I was glad when we needed to change buses.

"Wow, that was a loud ride. I am glad

we are off George's bus now," I said letting out a breath of relief.

"Is that bus usually that noisy?" Jack asked.

"No, there is normally a dull roar. But today it was almost like riding with a bunch of noisy kids," I explained laughing.

"Jack smiled and joined me. "Well, I am glad it is quiet now too."

"Here comes a bus, is that the one we need to take?" I asked.

"Yes, we are on States Street now so we just need to ride it about twelve blocks," he explained holding my hand.

"Cool," I said as we got on the bus and sat up close to the front so we could see out the front window.

Jack watched the addresses closely to make sure we got off at the stop closest to his address.

We got off the bus and walked back a block holding hands.

"I love you so much," he said looking over at me.

"I love you too," I said smiling as he gave my hand a gentle squeeze.

"We will walk up to the 2nd floor so we don't draw attention. Ok?" he informed me.

"Ok," I agreed.

"You will get to see the part I live in this time," he said as he opened the door.

"This is a different door. I went through that door the last time I was here," I said feeling confused.

"Right, when things were set up. My bosses told the management that they needed two apartments that were joined. Because they needed a front and back door," he explained as he opened the door

"Oh, then that makes sense," I said, "This is real nice.

"I wanted you to come here tonight. I figured we could just watch a little TV and eat in tonight. He said. "I'm cooking. Hope that is ok," he questioned.

"It sounds like a good evening," I said following him to the kitchen. "Wow, you have a lot of things to use I've never seen before. Can I help?" I asked.

"No, I get to do it all tonight, but I would love it if you wanted to stay in here with me and keep me company," he said giving me a kiss.

"Ok, I think I can do that," I said sitting down at the table.

Just then this very scruffy looking dog came walking into the kitchen. He is a strange-looking dog, on the smaller side of medium with floppy ears, eyes that were half hidden under multicolored hair that wasn't sure which direction it was supposed to grow.

"Oh that is Max, short for Maxamillion. He belongs to Andrew. He is about six months as far as I can tell," Jack informed me.

"Oh, sort of a strange-looking pup. But seems loving enough," I said while he licked my hand.

"Yes, Andrew found him sitting in the alley two building from here. He felt sorry for him and brought him back here," he said.

"So who is Andrew?" I questioned.

"Oh, he is one of our part-time travelers and drops in to help about every other week for a couple of days. So I guess Max is more mine now that his," he said laughing.

Max continued just sat next to me quietly watching Jack's every move, but not moving an inch.

"He is very well behaved," I said with a chuckle.

"Yes he is and the funny part is, I have never had to teach him anything. It is like he knows just what is required of him and when to do it," Jack said laughing.

"You have to say that is a great deal. I wonder if he likes cats?" I questioned while laughing. Max was tilting his head as if he understood what I had said.

"Dinner is almost ready," Jack said going to the refrigerator and brought out a small box.

"What is that?" I asked.

"It's a special food for Max. Andrew supplies it for me and left the instructions with me," he answered grabbing a spoon from the drawer. "So I dish out what Andrew said every evening about this time and if I am going to be out beyond this time then I put it out ahead of time. Max eats each night at the same time, the same amount," he added

"That sounds very strange," I said.

Jack put away the box back into the frig and took the plates out of the cabinet and dished out our dinners and put them on the table.

"It looks like a beef stew, but you cooked it so quickly. How?" I asked.

"I used a special cooker. It is one of the future gadgets that will help more people in the future to eat good when they are short on time. Andrew brought in to me one of the times he came though on a mission." He explained.

"The future is looking better and better every day," I said laughing.

"Oh talking about the future. I want to put a small tracker in your ring. Can you let me have it for a few minutes?" he asked.

"Ok," I said feeling a little confused. "Is something going to happen in the future that makes this needed?" I ask

"It's just a feeling I have and I have learned through the years to follow these feelings," he explained while I handed the ring and chain to him.

While Jack took the ring to his bedroom Max and I got a little more acquainted. "You look like a very special dog," I said.

Max tilted his head and let loud a sound that sounded like a quiet whimper then one eye blinked as if it was a wink. I caught myself as I giggle aloud as Max put one paw on my knee.

Just then Jack came walking back into the room. I see Max and you are getting along.

"Yes, Max is quite a dog and very smart," I said with a chuckle.

"He is very helpful. I am not sure how he learned to do all of the things he knows how to do, but he is a lot of company on quiet nights," Jack said while handing me back the chain and my ring.

"I'm looking at it but I am not seeing anything different. What did you do to it?" I asked taking a closer look.

"Ok, turn it so you can see the underside of the heart. Do you see the tiny black speck at the left-hand side edge of the heart?" He asked.

"Yes," I answered looking at it closer.

"Well that is the tracker," he explained. "You're getting ready to do to a very large city and things get lost and stolen easier in larger places. It's just a safety precaution I have a feeling that needed to be done," he explained.

"Ok," I said while putting the chain and ring back around my neck.

"What do you want to watch on TV? Any idea?" he asked as we walked into a cozy room with low lighting. He held out his hand toward a comfortable looking couch as he went over and turned on the TV. "I have a few movies too if you would rather," he offered.

"Do you have anything funny?" I asked.

"I have a lot of family type movies that have funny parts. I like the older ones like the one with the flying car or the candy factory or talking animals. I call them light entertainment but most of them give me a laugh every time I watch them" he explained.

"Then let's watch one of them," I said. "There is just too much junk on TV nowadays," I explained.

"Oh, I agree with you there," he said with a chuckle while putting the movie in the machine and pushing play.

We settled down and relaxed on the couch just as Max came into the room carrying a box of popcorn.

"Oh thanks, Max," Jack said taking it from him.

Then he looked over at me and started laughing.

I guess I was looking a little surprised and may have had my mouth open a little. Then I joined him in laughter. "But how…?" I started to say.

"Oh I buy the microwave popcorn by the box full and Max has learned how to open them and put them in the microwave and pushes a putting. It's not really that hard. As you can see the whole bag is in the box he brought in. He eats his part from the box," Jack explained laughing while taking the box from Max, opened the popcorn bag and poured some into the box. Then he sat the box next to Max on the couch.

"Max is a very smart dog," I said joining in the laughter.

After watching two movies, talking, laughing and snacking on popcorn, Jack looked at his watch.

"Oh my! Time flies when we are having fun. We only have about twenty minutes before the bus runs towards your place," he said after kissing me.

Max had been sitting on the couch with us. It was as if he understood everything that was being said. He jumped off the couch and ran for the door.

"You can't go Max, we have to catch a bus," Jack said.

Max dropped his head and walked slowly back to the couch.

"Did Andrew train him to be a service dog?" I asked.

"I don't think Andrew did much training with him at all. He just sort of knows what to do and when to do it," Jack answered slowly. "I hadn't really thought too much about it."

I grabbed my jacket as he opened the door.

We got to the bus stop with just enough time for a couple more kisses before the bus came to a stop.

Jack put our fares in the box and got two transfers. It wasn't long before we were standing at Nell's front door. I got one more kiss and a long hug before Nell opened the door.

"Hi Jack," Nell said with a big smile. "Do you want to come in for a little while?"

"No, I had better not. I need to catch the next bus heading towards my place," he explained, then he looked at his watch. "Well I guess I have a few minutes," he added while following me inside.

"Meow," Anna said running down the hall towards me.

"So this is Anna?" Jack said squatting down to pet her.

"Looks like she likes you," Nell said with a chuckle. "Would you like a drink? I have a cold one and also hot water ready for tea or coffee," she added.

"Oh maybe tea, tomorrow is to be a long day and I will need sleep tonight," he explained.

Jack drank his tea and Anna purred her loudest to make sure she had Jack's attention most of the time.

"Time is on the run again," Jack said looking at his watch. "The bus should be here in ten minutes. Oh Rita, I almost forgot to tell you that the apartment you told me about is in the right area."

I walked him to the door and stood on the front porch to wave as he rode past me.

"I hope he gets enough sleep tonight," I told Nell as we walked back into the house.

"I'm sure he will. It's only ten o five.

He should be home in plenty of time" she explained. "You worry too much," she added with a smile.

Chapter Nine

"We need to get into bed so we have enough rest. We both have work tomorrow," she said with a soft giggle as she closed her bedroom door.

Anna ran straight for the bedroom at that point and I followed. She was already curled up on her pillow by the time I got into bed.

"Good night Baby Girl," I said as I stroked her back.

And as she gave a soft meow we both closed our eyes.

Anna and I woke up the next morning to a very loud clanging noise.

I put on my robe and Anna followed me down the hall in the direction of the noise.

The scene in the kitchen was almost comical. There were pots and lids still rocking on the floor.

"What happened?" I asked looking at Nell and trying not to laugh.

"Oh, sorry about the noise, I wanted to

bake a cake today after work and was looking for a special pan of mine. But when I opened the cabinet I thought it was in all of the pans came flying out at the same time," she explained as we both started laughing.

"So, did you find the pan you were looking for?" I asked while helping to pick up the mess on the floor.

"No, but I found one that will do," she said as the last pan went back into the cabinet. "I wonder what I did with that cake pan?" she questioned thoughtfully.

"When did you buy it?" I asked

"Just the other day. It was cute and made me happy just looking at it," she explained.

"Maybe it is in your room. I've done that before. I mean, buy something then went in and changed and left the item on my bed," I suggested.

"Oh, could be," she said heading for her room.

"FOUND IT!" she yelled. "Yep, still in the bag and near my closet door," she informed me walking back into the kitchen holding up the bag.

"Take it out, I want to see what it looks like," I said.

"Oh, it's all balloons and flowers. Well, that makes it fun when it comes to icing it," I said laughing. "I like it. It is fun," I agreed.

"I thought so when I saw it. You want to help me make a cake tonight," she asked.

"For what?" I questioned.

"Oh no reason, just because I feel like having fun and this will be like having a coloring party," she reasoned.

"Ok, it sounds like fun. What food colorings do you have?" I asked.

"I'm not sure," she said opening up one of the drawers.

"I have blue, green, and red," she said holding them up.

"I can pick up a yellow after we get home. That will give Anna a chance to get out of the house. She loves going to Mr. Berealy's market," I offered.

"Ok, it's a deal. WE will have a great looking cake to eat tonight," she said laughing. "But right now we need to get ready for work. And we still have to eat yet. Cereal?" she questioned.

"Fine with me," I said while heading back to my room.

I hurried getting dressed hoping there would be enough time to call Ms. Beca March about the apartment.

When I got back to the kitchen Nell was setting up the table for breakfast. I hurried to the phone then looking at the clock. "Dang it, I can't call till later and I will be at work then," I muttered to myself.

"What are you mumbling about?" questioned Nell.

"Oh, I wanted to call Ms. Beca March and find out how large the apartment is that she has for rent. The one in San Francisco I told you about," I explained. "But it is too early there for me to call. It's only four-thirty A.M. there. I don't think I want to wake up my new landlord to ask questions about an apartment I don't have yet," I said laughing.

"I agree, I don't think I would want to be woke up that early either," Nell said laughing as she sat down to eat.

I joined her at the table and as I took my last few bites, she hurried off to put on her makeup. "I'm still glad I don't wear makeup," I said looking down at Anna, who was asking for the last of the milk in my bowl.

I got up poured it into her dish, washed the dishes and cleaned the kitchen. Then I slicked my hair back into a ponytail while I waited for Nell to finish. We still had about twelve minutes before George would be coming by. I figured I would start the countdown in about three minutes. That way we still had time to get to the bus stop in time.

Just I got ready to say "Times up ready or not" Nell came out of the bathroom.

"Let's get. Time is ticking," she said laughing.

"Be good Anna, see you after work," I said grabbing my jacket and running for the door.

Nell was already standing in the door ready to lock it when I got to it.

"Race you," she said as we were fast walking.

"Ok," and I started running.

We laughed all the way there. But we made it about two minutes before George.

"Good morning George," I said as I let him punch my bus pass.

"Thank you and thanks for the race," he said looking at both of us and chuckled.

Nell dropped her coins in the box and we headed for our favorite seats.

"Oh, I almost forgot," Nell said looking through her purse. "Here are the pictures of your paintings you asked me to do the other day." She said handing them to me.

"Thanks now I can show Charlie," I said taking them from her and putting them in my jacket pocket.

"Why did he need to see what you are painting?" Nell asked.

"He said something about hanging a few one of the other ways," I said shrugging my shoulders.

"Oh well that's nice," she said looking forward as a disturbance a few seats in front of us. "I think there may be trouble on our little peaceful bus," she whispers through cupped hands.

"The guy in the red shirt just got on the stop after ours and the other guy was already on the bus," I whispered to Nell.

"I know but I have a feeling there is going to be a big fight soon," she said

Just then the one in the red shirt pulled a large knife and lunged at the guy next to him. Then there was the firing of a gun.

"Oh my gosh," was that a gunshot we just heard?" I asked Nell.

"I think it was. Get down behind the seat as close to the floor as you can," she said.

We both scrunched down as close to the floor as we could.

"Maybe he won't see us," she whispered.

"STOP THE BUS!" came the voice of the other guy that had been sitting there first.

"I can see his feet. He is at the back door," I whispered to Nell.

"Shhhh, " she said quietly.

George pulled over the bus in the middle of the block and the guy pushed hard on the doors and they finally opened.

"Dispatch? Call 911. There was a shooting on my bus. I am in the middle of the block of Juniper Street," George yelled.

Then he rushed back to the guy that had been shot to see if he could help.

"Is there a doctor, medic or nurse on board?" he yelled.

A nurse raised her hand.

"Please come see what you can do to help this guy while I flag down a policeman," he instructed. "Everyone else please stay calm and seated," he said while going out the back door of the bus.

We got off the floor and sat down in our seats. We looked around to see where we were and how far I was from the Rooster.

"Looks like we are about halfway on our ride to the Rooster," I said.

"Yep, too far to walk. Besides the police is going to ask for a description of the guy that did the shooting," Nell informed me.

I looked over at the door. "They should be able to find him. He's bleeding," I said.

"Why do you say that?" she questioned.

"There are blood shears on the doors where he was pushing on them," I said pointing at the door.

"Oh yeah, I see them now," she said. "We may as well just sit back and figure we will be here for a while," she said.

"True," I said taking a deep breath and pulled out the pictures that Nell had handed me earlier.

"I think they look better in pictures than for real," I said laughing quietly

"No, they look the same," she said joining me with a soft snicker.

"Oh Nell, do you by chance have a piece of paper in your purse?" I asked.

"Maybe, why?" she asked.

"I thought I would sketch the other guy's shoes while I am sitting here before I forget anything," I answered quietly.

"Good idea," she said looking through her purse and pockets "It seems all I have is the back of an old grocery list," she said handing it to me.

"That will do. Thanks," I said as I took it.

George came back with two police officers. They both had out their notebooks and pens. As they went through everyone on the bus asking questions we found out that the man just in front of us had been eavesdropping on their conversation. It seemed it was about money due on a loan. But he didn't see who it was that was talking. So couldn't say who made the loan. Meanwhile, the ambulance had come and carried the injured guy away. After each person had talked to the police they were asked to stand outside of the bus. I gave them the drawing of the shoes and I was told that may help.

It seemed that the dispatch was sending another bus to take this ones place

We went over and stood next to George. He was still a little pale for all that had happened.

"How are you two doing?" he asked.

"We are fine. Question is how are you doing?" we asked almost in unison.

"A little better than I was now that there is a different bus coming for me to drive. The medics that were here said I was good to finish my day," he reported.

"Oh good then we won't have a stranger taking us home tonight," we said together then started laughing.

"It looks like the two of you are going

to be late to work," he said.

"True but I think we will be forgiven," I said pointing to the TV crew that had just shown up. "They are head for you," I said in almost a singing tone.

"Oh Boy, like I really needed this today," he said giving out a long breath.

"Let's stand behind him so Charlie and your boss can see we were really on this bus," I whispered quietly to Nell.

She nodded.

While the TV cameras were on George, we made sure that we got in the scene as proof we were in the middle of all that had gone down and gave a small wave so we would be seen.

Just as the TV crew moved on to other people the other bus drove up.

George waved to everyone's attention that had been on his bus. "Everyone, the bus is here. It's time to get everyone to where they were going before all of this went down," he yelled to get above all of the street noise.

We all took our seats in the same place we were before everything went down. That is except one guy that was arguing with George about being on the bus before.

Before letting him on, George asked. "Who were you sitting close to?"

"I was sitting next to a guy with a plaid shirt," he said sounding angry.

"I only had one person that changed their mind about continuing their ride. So let's see if any of the people remember seeing you," George said.

Chapter Ten

"Ok, so I don't have enough money. But I need to get to this job interview," he said in almost a begging manner.

"You know I shouldn't even let you on the bus for lying to start with," George said. "So how much money do you have and how far did you need to go?"

"I only have one dollar and I think fifty-six cents," he said digging through all of his pockets. "And I need to get to Spectrum Street," he added holding out everything he had.

"Well, you know that you are a little over seventy-five cents short. I will loan it to you but I need something to hold till you pay me back," George said. "It's not the money it is the way you went about it."

"I have a nice pocket knife and a new yoyo," he said offering them to George.

"I will hold the pocket knife, but why do you have a yoyo?" George asked.

"It helps me un-stress," he answered.

"Ok, well you sit right here, so I can tell you when to get off," George instructed pointing to the front seat across from him.

The guy sat down and we were soon on our way again.

Soon George slowed down and stopped just a couple of stops before mine.

"What is your name? This is your stop," George asked.

"Oh sorry, Sammy. Sammy Trackle," he said.

"Take this transfer and walk three blocks that way and catch the 42nd bus northbound," George instructed. "And don't try the stunt you tried with me on anyone else."

"Oh I won't and thank you for the help," Sammy said while getting off the bus.

We moved up to the front so we could see how George was doing.

"Boy what a day and it isn't even half over yet," George said as we sat down across from him.

We hear that. And it all went down just a few seats in front of us," Nell and I said almost in unison, then giggle softly at each other. Not that all that had happened so far was funny but that we were saying the same thing at the same time again, and for us that was always funny.

It didn't take long and we were at my stop. "See you later George," I said while he opened the door and gave Nell a short wave as I got off.

I just know I have some explaining to do when I get to work. After all, I'm almost three hours late.

"Hi Joy, is Charlie in his Office?" I asked as I came through the door.

"Sure. HAY CHARLIE, OUR TV STAR IS HERE!" she announced the laughing, "Yeah one of our customers told us they had seen you on the TV New Flash. So is that wild of what?" she asked.

"It was very strange," I said.

Charlie walked up just then. "Well? What is your excuse for being late?" he asked trying to hold back a chuckle.

"Well, Nell and I were on the bus talking when this young guy, I would say maybe around twenty-two years old sat down next to this older guy and started yelling. They both got loud. It seems the younger one loaned money to the older one and the older one refused to pay. The young one pulled a really large knife out of his backpack and stabbed the older one. The older one shot the younger one then forced George to stop and he pushed the doors open and ran. I got a good look at his shoes so I drew a picture of them and gave it to the police," I explained. "And that is why I am late getting to work," I added.

Charlie just chuckled, "Well you are here now, so get to work. Even TV stars have to work," he said laughing while we walked back to his office.

The rest of the day went fast. I was

surprised as to how many people managed to watch TV New Flashes or hear about them from friends.

On the way home Nell and I compared our workday as to how many people mentioned seeing the TV News Flashes.

The phone was ringing as we walked through the door. Nell answered it as I headed for my room to change close with Anna close on my heels.

"It's for you Rita," Ness shouted from the kitchen. "It's Jack." She added handing me the phone.

"Hi Jack," I said

"Are you and Nell ok? I saw the news flash earlier today," he asked.

"Oh yeah, we are ok. I was just late getting to work. But everything worked out ok. Oh dang it, I forgot to give the pictures of my art to Charlie to look at. And can I call you back in a little bit? I need to talk to Beca in San Francisco real quick?" I asked.

"Sure, how about I call you back in about an hour?" he asked.

"Ok, that will work too," I said. "Bye, I love you, talk to you in a little bit" I add before hanging up the phone.

I looked through my pockets for Beca's phone number. 'I must have left it on the dresser,' I thought heading for the bedroom.

'Yep, here it is. Good, I hope that the room is large enough,' I thought while going back to the kitchen to call.

"Hello Beca, This is Rita. Rita Stolks. I've talked to you about renting one of your rooms," I said hoping she remembered me.

"Oh Yes, I remember you. How can I help you?" she asked.

"Well, when we talked last I forgot to ask how large the room is?" I asked.

"Oh, I'm sure you will like it. It measures twelve feet by twenty feet not counting the bathroom. Oh and there is a small out cove for sitting on warm nights," she explained.

"That sounds perfect. I sent off the check for the amount you asked for yesterday," I informed her.

"That is lovely dear. I will have your keys waiting for you when you get into town. Is that all you wanted to know?" she asked.

"Yes, that was all I wanted," I said relieved to hear that is as large as it was. "Thank you and good night," I said hanging up the phone.

"Guess what Nell?" I said feeling excited.

"What?" Nell said while putting on hotdogs for dinner.

"The place in San Francisco is a twelve by fourteen feet with a small porch and storage in the basement," I explained almost jumping with excitement.

"Oh, that is a good size. When do you plan to leave for San Francisco?" she asked.

"Well I sort of gave Charlie my about

a week ago," I said looking at the floor.

"What do you mean sort of?" she asked with a chuckle.

"Well, I told him I was going to go to San Francisco to learn to paint like my sister soon. He didn't ask me when or how soon. Instead, that is when he asked to see pictures of what I had been painting," I explained.

"Well that is not really a notice. He may want it in writing. Better ask him tomorrow. So some is your rent started on the apartment?" she asked.

"Oh, my gosh. It starts in about two weeks," I answered just realizing that time was getting away from me.

"You know that it will take you several days to get there riding the bus. Don't you? So you may want to let him know tomorrow," she suggested.

"I can do that, but I want to show him the pictures of my art first," I said laughing.

Anna was now wrapping herself around my feet and meowing like she was starving and unloved.

"Oh I know baby girl, I am sorry. I didn't greet you when I first got home. You would not believe all that happened today," I said picking her up and hugging her with a few stroked along her back. It didn't take much for her to purr. She is such a good friend.

"We have to get you a pet carrier so I can take you on the bus with me," I told her while petting her some more.

I put her down on the chair so I could answer the phone. "Hello?" I said.

"Rita, it me, Jack. So did you find out how big your new place is going to be?" he asked.

"Yes and it is even larger than my old apartment without the walls," I answered laughing. "Oh and it has a little sitting porch," I added.

"That sounds real nice. I just may have to take a try and see it after you get settled in. Are we still on for tomorrow night?" he asked.

"Sure, what are we going to do?" I asked.

"Well, pretty much anything you want. We can eat out and go dancing. Or eat in and watch movies. I still have a lot you haven't seen yet. Or we could eat out and go to the movies. Your choice," he offered.

"I don't really know what I will be in the mood for tomorrow," I said laughing. "Can I see how tomorrow goes?" I asked.

"Sure, my queen so whatever you decide, we can do. Ok?" he said.

"Goodnight, Love you," I said.

"Goodnight Love, see you tomorrow after work," he said and then hung up.

"Good, just in time," Nell said. "Dinner is on the table," she added as I turned around and we both started laughing.

"Wow, what a day. This is going to make the rest of the week seem dull," I said.

"Yes, and I hope it does," Nell said

continuing the laughter.

We ate dinner then watched a little TV. Then just before we turned off the TV the News came on. "Well I guess we can stay up long enough to see how everything came out today," she said.

"True," I said as we sat back down.

"Oh no! They didn't catch the guy with the gun," I said.

"I think everything will be ok. We were behind the seats when he got up to leave," Nell reminded me.

"True, but this look we were on TV standing behind George," I said getting a little worried.

"Don't worry, He's not going to come looking for us just because we were showing off behind George. People are always doing that when there is a TV camera around. That won't mean anything to this guy," Nell reassured me.

"Ok, if you think we will be ok," I said still feeling a little shaky.

"I am sure. There is nothing to worry about," she said as we went to our rooms. Good night, Sweet Dreams," she said

"MEOW," Anna said.

"Oh and to you too Anna," Nell said with a slight chuckle.

"Good night Nell," I said as I closed the door.

The morning bustle the city woke me as it came through my window.

"How did you sleep Anna?" I asked as

I turned to face her.

She gave a big yawned, did a long stretch the jumped off the bed heading for the door.

"Well, you are going to have to wait a few minutes because I am not quite as fast as you this morning. I guess that happened yesterday took more energy than I thought. I must have tossed and turned all night. I feel really tier this morning," I said as I yawned.

I managed to get out of bed and dressed. After all, I had things that I needed to do today. First of all feed Anna. She was underfoot wrapping around my legs reminding me she hadn't eaten yet.

"You make me laugh baby girl. You are such a good baby," I said opening the door and heading for the kitchen.

"Good morning, how did you sleep last night?" Nell asked as we walked into the kitchen.

"Not too well I guess. I am really tired this morning," I said while getting Anna taken care of.

"Me too. That is why I like coffee," Nell laughed.

"I like the smell but not the taste," I said joining her in laughter.

"Well, the multivitamins are on the table. I took mine already," she said while buttering the toast.

I laid them out next to my bowl that was already on the table. Then I spotted the pot on the stove. I walked over and grabbed the spoon, took off the lid and figured on stirring oatmeal. "Oh, you changed it up this morning. It's cream of wheat," I exclaimed with a chuckle.

"I figured we needed something different than we normally eat. So there are no eggs or oatmeal this morning. But we do have fruit," she offered. "Strawberries, apples or raisins," she added.

I glanced at the clock. "Good we have a little over half of an hour before George comes by," I said.

"Good, that is just enough time for me to get everything done I need to before leaving," she said with a giggle.

After eating she went to do her makeup while I did the dishes and straightened up the kitchen and took out a few minutes to visit with Anna.

"Ready to go?" Nell asked as she came out of her room.

"Yep, just finished," I said.

I grabbed my jacket and felt the pocket to make sure the pictures were in it that I wanted to shoe Charlie today.

We hurried out the door and down the steps and I spotted George about three blocks away.

"We have to run this morning," I said.

"I'm going to win," Nell shouted as she took off like a rocket.

George managed to make it to the bus stop a few seconds before me. Nell got there just before he managed to stop.

"Well I beat at least one of you," he laughed.

"Good morning George," Nell and I said in almost unison. Then the laughter started.

"How long do you get to keep this new bus, George?" I asked.

"From now on I hope. It has all of the modern stuff, like cameras and lots of lights," he said laughing.

"I agree and it's real pretty. I like the colors," I said as we turned to head for our seat in the back.

It didn't seem to take long before we were closing in on my stop.

"See you after work," I told Nell as I got up and headed for the back door.

"George stopped the bus and as I got off I yelled, "See you later George," with a wave.

As I walked to The Rooster I felt my pocket again to make sure that the pictures were still there.

As I walked through the door Sandy was at the front counter.

"Hi Sandy, Where is Charlie?" I asked.

"In the kitchen, I think," she said pouring more coffee for a customer.

I went around the counter and headed for the kitchen.

He and Jimmy were fixing something on the dishwasher. There was water all over the floor.

"Oh my. What happened? I asked.

"Oh, hi Rita. One of the hoses came loose. Well, that is what we thought it was at first. But after looking at it we found a small hole in it. So we cut it back and now we are trying to get it to stretch far enough to make it hold," Charlie explained.

Jimmy just stood them with a big gin on his face. He and I both knew that he had been trying to talk Charlie into buying a new dishwasher for a few years without getting anywhere.

"Did you need something Rita?" he asked looking over his shoulder at me.

"I have those pictures you wanted to see of my paintings. There was so much happening yesterday that I forgot about them till after I was already home," I said.

"Ok, well, I will be with you in a few minutes. Just as soon as I get done here, I think we just about have this fixed," he said sticking his head and both arms back into the dishwashing machine.

"Wait in my office for me. I should be there in a few minutes," came his muffled voice from inside.

"Ok," I said as I left the kitchen and walked toward his office, but decided at the last minutes to get a quick soda.

I went back to his office and laid the pictures out on his desk.

Chapter Eleven

"Here they are," I said proudly. While

     I laid all of the pictures out on his desk
for him to take a look at.
     "Oh my, I didn't know you had
already painted this many pictures. It seems

you have been real busy," he said smiling. "Can I keep these for a while? I want to be able to study them before picking the ones I want to hang in the dining room," he added.

"Ok maybe you can let me know before I leave work today," I said as I put on my apron.

"Sure, ok," Charlie said seemingly distracted by another note he found on his desk.

The day went by fast and sat down for a few minutes waiting on George to come in for his coffee. Then I remembered that Charlie had my pictures.

I walked by to his office. "Hey Charlie," I said as I got closer to his office.

There was no answer. As I got to his office I could see he wasn't in it. "Jimmy where is Charlie? Do you know?" I asked turning to face the kitchen.

"I'm not real sure. He said something about the whole sellers. I guess that is where he went," Jimmy answered while spraying off the plates.

"Ok. Well when he gets back tell him I will check with him tomorrow about what he thought about the pictures he was looking at earlier today," I said.

"I can do that. But I can tell you which ones I liked. I took a peek while on my lunch break," he said laughing.

"Oh? So which ones?" I asked while keeping an ear open for George.

"I like the rooms. I think we should

make a couple of them really big so it looks like we've added a few rooms to the café," he said giving me his mischievous laugh and sort of wringing his hands.

I had to join in his laughter when he did that laugh. It reminded me sort of the mad scientist in the older movies.

"George is here," Betty yelled.

"Be right there," I said loudly on my way back to the front.

"Hi, George. Are you ready? Got your coffee?" I asked grabbing my jacket.

"Nope, we have a couple of minutes," he said sitting down on one of the stools as Betty put his coffee on the counter.

"Ok," I said grabbing myself a small soda.

"So what was Jimmy doing his mad scientist laugh about?" questioned Betty.

"Oh I left some pictures of my painting with Charlie earlier this morning and Jimmy saw them. He was saying that he liked the rooms," I replied with a chuckle. "He wants to make it really large," I added.

"Interesting," she said as she went to wait on the few customers that just came in.

"Ready to go Rita?" George said.

"Sure," I said as I followed him out to the bus. I was still thinking about the idea of making one of my rooms larger. I paid my fare and found Nell and sat down.

"What's up? You look like you are in another world," Nell said.

"Oh, just thinking about something

that Jimmy said before I left work," I said

Then I explained all that had happened that day on our way home.

'Here is our stop," Nell said.

"See you tomorrow," I yelled to George as we got off.

Nell grabbed the mail on our way up the steps. She opened the door and I headed for my bedroom with Anna on my heels.

Anna jumped onto the bed and sat there watching while I emptied my pockets and changed clothes, giving me a meow here and there.

Then she jumped down and ran for the kitchen. I followed knowing that she was most likely headed for the refrigerator. As I rounded the corner, sure enough, there she sat in front of the refrigerator door looking up at the handle.

"Ok, I'm here. Do you know what you want before I open the frig?" I questioned.

"Meow," she said looking at me then back at the refrigerator.

I had to laugh, "Ok baby girl. I'll open it. You know where your food is," I said.

As soon as I opened it she put one paw on her food and the other on her milk container.

"I see you have it all figured out. You want both today. Well ok, it looks like you finished all of your dry food earlier today," I laughed while taking the food to the counter. I got out her dish and placed it on the floor just as Nell came into the kitchen.

"Here," she said handing me an envelope. "It looks like it is from the insurance co your landlord had."

"Oh good, maybe it is enough to pay for the bus trip to San Francisco. Jack and I had planned to go to the pet store tomorrow and pick out a pet carrier so I can take Anna with me. I sent off the check for rent to Beca the other day. So I have a place to live in almost three weeks. I planned to officially tell Charlie tomorrow. That gives him the two-week notice.

"What about Jack? I mean you out there and him being stuck in a job here," Nell questioned.

"It will be hard for a little while. Jack and I are hoping that his bosses will understand and that maybe they will transfer him to their San Francisco base. If not, we will have to figure out another way to work all of this out," I explained while opening the envelope.

I guess my eyes got wide and my mouth must have dropped open. "What? How much did they give you?" Nell insisted. "Tell me I can hardly wait."

"The check is for over a thousand dollars. The letter says "This amount is to cover two months' rent and the rest is to compensate for the loss of personal keepsakes. We were informed that nothing in the building can be retrieved without danger," I read aloud. "This is wonderful. This means I can get a bed and whatever else

I will need when I get to San Francisco."

"That is great. I'm glad they gave you something to cover the cost of replacing other things you had," Nell said. "Let's have something easy for dinner tonight," she added.

"Hum, maybe tuna and egg salad sandwiches?" I questioned.

"That sounds fine. And I'm sure that Anna won't turn down any leftovers," she said with a chuckle. And we both broke into laughter when we noticed that Anna was paying close attention to what we were saying.

"I'll get the eggs started. I figure about four, will that be enough you think?" I asked.

"I'm pretty sure that will be enough. Here is the steamer pot," Nell announced handing me the pop.

I guess I looked a little confused.

"Steaming the eggs for about sixteen minutes works real good. Then you dump them into ice water to make the shells turn loose," she instructed.

"Ok, this will be my first time steaming eggs," Then I thought about it for a few seconds. "Oh! This is like poaching them but longer," I said as the light went on with laughter following.

'Yep, one of my chef friends told me about it. He said it saves him a lot of time," she explained.

"What's on TV tonight?" I asked.

"That show you said you wanted to

watch last week when you saw the commercial. We should have finished eating and the cleanup done by the time it comes on," she encouraged.

"Oh good. I'm glad you remembered. I had forgotten what day it was to come on," I confessed.

"Here Anna, something to keep you busy for a few minutes," Nell said laughing as she gave Anna the tuna can to lick and play with till we were finished eating.

I joined in. Anna was one of the few cats that didn't pay attention to people laughing when she was around. My uncle once told me that cats hate being laughed at. But Anna didn't seem to mind. But I was always laughing about something. Laughter helps heal the body and keep the mind sharp.

"Let's eat while she is busy," Nell said giving me a slight nudge while sitting down at the table.

It didn't take us long before we had finished our sandwiches and drinks.

"Let's get the kitchen clean so we can enjoy the rest of our night," Nell urged.

"Oh, we need to hurry. It's later than we thought," I said after glancing at the kitchen clock.

"Oh, I agree," Nell said after looking up from cleaning the table.

We finished with just enough time to refill our drinks, give Anna the leftovers and head to the living room.

Nell turned on the TV as she went by. We sat down and got comfortable. It didn't take long before Ann came running in and curled up beside me on the couch.

"Have you given you notice to Charlie yet?" Nell asked during a commercial.

"No I was going to today but I didn't get the chance. I will try again tomorrow," I answered quickly.

"That was interesting but long," I said with a yawn.

"Yes I agree, but pilots for new programs are normally long. Next week it may only be half an hour," she said turning off the TV.

"Well good night. Sleep well," I said heading for my bedroom with Anna leading the way.

"Good night," she said laughing. Ann almost looked as if she was proudly prancing.

"Meow, Meow," Anna said putting her paw on my cheek.

"Well good morning to you too," I said opening my eyes to see her almost nose to nose with me. I had to laugh. "Your such a good friend. Let me get dressed and then we can eat," I added.

"Good morning," Nell called out as we passed her bedroom.

"Good morning," I replied with Anna joining in with her own greeting a long drawn out "M-e-o-w."

"And good morning to you Anna,"

Nell said with a chuckle.

Anna headed straight for the frig. I checked her bowl as I passed by and it was completely clean

"I'm getting there," I said while stopping to get me a glass. "I know you're hungry," I said reaching for the refrigerator door. "I see you know what you want and you are fast about pointing it out," I added while taking out the milk and her can of food.

"Here you are baby girl," I said putting her food in her bowls and petting her as Nell walked in.

"You're two are up early today," she said

"Yeah, Anna woke up hungry this morning," I said laughing.

"Cereal ok this morning?" Nell asked.

"Sure, hot or cold?" I asked

"I was thinking cold," Nell replied.

"Ok," I said grabbing two bowls.

Nell grabbed the cereal and I out the milk and both glasses on the table.

After what seemed to be only a few minutes, "OH my gosh! Time is flying at top speed today," Nell blurted, as she put her bowl in the sink and almost ran for the bathroom.

"Sure looks like it," I agreed while taking the glasses and my bowl to the sink.

Anna was wrapping her tail around my legs asking for attention.

I sat down for a few minutes and

petted her while the sink was being prepped for washing dishes.

I just finish the dishes and cleaning off the cabinets and had set up Anna's food for while we were gone as Nell came out of the bathroom.

She glanced at the clock and almost screamed, "We have to run and I mean now!"

"By baby girl see you when I get home," I told Anna while grabbing my jacket.

Nell already had the door open and was waiting on my.

As we ran down the steps and out to the bus stop, I said almost laughing, "One of these days I would like to know what it feels like to walk to the bus stop."

"I know what you mean but you know it does get the blood pumping for the day," Nell laughed.

"Hi George," we said almost in unison then the laughter was ever stronger.

"Hello girls. I think today was a tie," Chuckled George.

"I was close," Nell said and we laughed all the way to our usual seats.

It didn't take long before it was time for me to get off.

"By Nell," then I gave a wave to George, "See you later George," I yelled while stepping off the bus.

Charlie caught me just as I walked through the door, "Come in the office. I have a few questions," he said in his serious voice.

Sandy said in almost a whisper, "Oh oh."

I gave her a wink and followed Charlie to his office.

I've been looking at your pictures and I think I like this one, he said pointing to the room with the fish. But I want it a lot larger than I think you originally painted it. What do you think?"

"What size are you talking about?" I asked wondering if Jimmy had mentioned his idea.

"Can you paint it on the wall and make a few changes while you are at it?' He asked "I would like it to look like another room they could walk into from a distance. Can you do that ?" he added.

"I'm pretty sure I can. At least I will give it my best try." I answered thinking this would be the challenge of my life. "Ok, I will paint this for you as my last act here. After that, I have plans to head to San Francisco to follow in my sister's footsteps." I added.

"So is this like a two-week notice?" he questioned with a slight chuckle.

"Yes, but what is so funny?" I asked.

"I kind of thought you would. After all the money she got for just one painting. Wow!" he said laughing. "We will all miss you. Now, the changes I want in the painting. I want the table over here in the pic and the stand over there," he said pointing.

"I'm sure I can so that," I said, taking the pictures and walking back out to the front to help Sandy with the customers.

"What did he want," Sandy asked in a quiet voice.

"Oh he wanted to tell me which of my paintings he wanted on the wall," I said while putting on my apron.

The day went by fast and I had just put things away and grabbed my jacket as Jack walked through the door.

"Your timing is great. But I just thought of a question I have for Charlie. So wait right here please," I said running towards Charlie's office.

"Charlie, I have a question. Are you paying for the paint for this wall painting you want? We didn't talk about any of that," I said.

"Let me think about it and I will let you know in the morning," he said looking at his desk.

"Ok," I said and went back to where Jack was standing.

"Ready to go?" Jack asked.

"Yes I want to go to the mall and see if we can find a pet carrier," I said as we walked out the door.

"I know just the place," he said. "Run and we can catch this bus then transfer," he added.

"Hi George, I got off a little early today," I said.

"And we will need two transfers

please," Jack added with a smile.

George handed Jack the transfers and we sat down just across from George.

"What happened at work today? Did you give your notice?" Jack asked.

"Yes but not before he asked me to paint a wall mural for him, of one of my paintings," I replied.

"I hope he is paying for the paint and supplies. And then pays you for painting it," Jack said.

"I asked but didn't get an answer. He said he would have to figure it out," I informed him.

"Well, I'm sure he will do right by you," Jack said looking out the window. "We will need to get off in about another four blocks," he added giving my hand a gentle squeeze.

"George, we will need to get off around Murphy Street," I said getting George's attention.

"Ok," he replies smiling but keeping his eyes on the road.

"Here's your stop. If you hurry you can catch the next bus over there," George said pointing across the street.

Chapter Twelve

"This is your stop. Remember THE LAST round I make is at nine tonight," he reminded me.

"I'm not sure just what all we are going to be doing tonight. But I will see you tomorrow," I said with a wave as we got off the bus.

After George drove away, we went across the street to the other bus stop.

"Where are we going?" I asked

"I know of a pet supply store on Queens Blvd. I think you will find what you will like there. You're looking for a nice carrier so you can take Anna with you right?" he asked to confirm with a chuckle.

"Yes, I figure that to may take me the next two weeks just to paint the mural Charlie wants and I'm going to try and get packed during that time. I bought our bus tickets already. Anna gets to travel for a child's seat. That way I don't have to hold the carried only lap the whole way," I explained.

"That was good thinking and did they give you the discount for buying so far ahead?" he asked.

"Yes, I saved enough to pay for our food all the way there," I said as we both started laughing.

"Here comes the bus," Jack announced. "There are a few places we can look in to find just the right carrier for Anna," he added as the bus came to a stop.

"Hello," Jacks said, "I think we will need another transfer."

"Where are you trying to go?" asked the bus driver.

"Pet supplies on Queens Blvd," Jack explained.

"Then yes you will need one more transfer. I will let you know when we get close to your stop," the bus driver replied.

"Thank you, " I said as I took the transfers and we sat down across from the drive.

It wasn't long before the driver said. "This will be your stop. You will need to catch the bus over there on that side and ride for about another ten blocks."

"Thank you we both said at the same time, and that started us laughing as we got off the bus.

We waited for the light to change before crossing to the bus stop. Just as we got ready to sit down Jack spotted the bus.

"That was quick," I laughed.

Jack took my hand and we got on the

bus, handed off our transfers, and sat up close to the front so we could see the road. We didn't want to miss our stop.

Jack spotted the store and pulled the cord and as it gave a ding I grabbed it and gave it a tug too. "I always wanted to do that," I said with a big grin and a chuckle.

The bus stopped we said thank you and got off by the front door.

"This store is huge. I'm sure it should have the carrier I need for Anna," I said taking hold of Jack's hand.

As we walked through the doors I had to say, "Oh, my gosh Jack. Look at all of these things. We have to take time just to look at all of this while we are here. Ok?"

"Sure that is why I wanted to take you here. I figured this place would have just what you need and want," he said. "Here take the shopping cart and let's stroll around and look at everything," he added.

"Oh, it's a whole aisle full of toys for cats. They are on both sides. I think I will get her a few new ones. Maybe they will keep her occupied on the long bus ride," I said looking through all of the things hanging in front of me. "Oh look at all of the treats. Oh my goodness, this is so cute," I said picking up a few other things.

"I can see I may need to hold on to the breaks," Jack said laughing.

"What?" I questioned.

"After you get through loading the shopping cart, I will be asking a few questions," he said laughing and putting his hands in his pockets.

"Ok, I think I see what you are saying. But this is so exciting. I guess I am like turning a kid loose in a candy shop," I confessed.

"Well, yeah, sort of," he said laughing.

After going through the whole isle, I did have almost half a cart filled with toys, treats and can food.

"Ok, here are the questions I wanted to ask you. How many days and nights will you be on the bus getting to San Francisco?" Jack asked.

"I was told that it would take about three to four days depending on the roads," I answered. Wondering where Jack was alluding to.

"Well, I was thinking maybe only get one toy for each day and maybe only two bags of treats. She may not feel too much like eating or playing, after all, she will be in a new place, and strange noises," he said.

"Oh that's true," I said looking through all of the things I had picked out.

"Uh, these are for the trip and these three are for after we get there," I said placing all of them in the upper part of that cart.

"Then we need to put these back," he said laughing.

"True, ok," I said joining the laughter. "Let's go look at the carriers before I add anything else," I added.

"Ok, according to the little map I found as we walked in, they should be on isle fifteen, that way," he said pointing with a chuckle.

"Good," I said pushing the cart down to the end of the aisle and turning left. "Oh look there are bed pads and baskets and little houses. This place has everything one could imagine," I said pointing out things as we worked our way to isle fifteen.

"Wow! Look at all the different kinds of pet carriers there are. I didn't know that they made this many," I almost shouted in excitement.

"That is the reason why we are here," Jack laughed.

It took me a while to look at all of the carriers in the size I would need. But I finally settled on one style, now it was just a matter of picking the color.

"I think I like the burnt orange carrier with the black netting. It will match Anna's fur," I said with a giggle. "The other part I like is that it has a zipper opening in the top while a cuff, so I can open it and pet her while we are traveling and she can't get out that way with my hand in the way. And the front door has a double latch" I added.

"Did you notice that there are pockets on the outside for toys, a water bottle, and a few other things?" Jack asked.

"Oh, nice. I just got to thinking I will need a harness and leash, so when we stop I can let her out for a walk and potty break," I said.

"I found the leashes and harness. They are over there," Jack said pointing to the other side of the aisle.

I put the carrier in the shopping cart along with the other things I planned to buy.

"I like this set," I said holding up a soft harness and a long leash made of a material that changes color from blue to purple. "It is really pretty," I added.

"I agree," Jack said. "Is this all that you will need for Anna on the trip?" he asked

"I should get some canned food to take along on the trip," I replied.

"Jack looked at the map, then pointing to it said, "Cat food is all on aisle twelve."

As we walked down aisle twelve I felt amazed at how many brands and the different kinds of packaging that was available.

I looked over each one and then I spotted the one I wanted to get. It's the kind she's used to eating. But instead of it being in cans they were in soft pouches. That'll make them easier to pack.

"I think this will do it for the trip," I said put four, six-packs into the cart.

"Are you ready to go then?" Jack asked with a big smile.

"Yes I think so," I said looking over all of the things I had in the cart.

"Good, cause I 'm starting to get hungry," he said with a chuckle.

"Me too, come to think about it. Is there a place you know about in this area?" I asked laughing.

"Hum, you know I think there is. Let's check out and then we can go see," he said while helping me put everything on the check-out counter.

Once we got everything I had bought put into the carrier, we walked out the front doors.

Jack acted like he was thinking really hard, then, "Ah-ha. I think if we were to walk this way I'm sure we will find a good steak house in the next block. Hand me the carrier and I will carry it. These blocks are pretty long."

"This is turning out to be such a great day. I mean I got the things I needed to take Anna with me on the bus and now a good dinner. Oh and I don't want to forget that Charlie asked me to paint a full wall mural of my fish room." I explained.

"While we wait on our food, maybe you can show me the picture you are doing the mural of," Jack suggested.

"Sure and I will tell you the changes he wants done in it. So it won't be just like the one I originally painted," I explained.

"Good, here we are," he said opening the door for me.

We headed straight for a booth. That way I could put the carrier in the corner.

After we ordered I took the pictures out of my jacket pocket.

"Here is the one he wants me to paint on the back wall for him. It is to look like the café has added a new room when I get through with it. This is it," I said putting it out on the table.

"Well, here it is," I said pushing it across the table to him.

"Wow, this is amazing. It looks like you could really walk into the room," Jack said taking a closer look at it. "This is nice. I didn't know you could paint this good," he added.

It wasn't long before we had finished our meal and started back to Nell's house.

"Do you want to come in for a cup of coffee and maybe some apple crumb cake?" I asked.

"Well maybe, but just for a few minutes. I want to be able to catch the next but," Jack answered as Nell opened the door.

"How did it go? Oh, wow. That is a nice carrier," she said noticing the carried as Jack carried it into the house.

"I found so many things. That is such a large store. It's like a big warehouse and it is packed full," I informed her on our way to the kitchen. "I offered Jack coffee and crumb cake. And I can give him that," I added.

"I put the wafer on for coffee a few minutes ago," Nell replied.

Jack put the carried in one corner of the kitchen and Anna found it right away. I walked over to pet her after giving Jack a piece of cake.

"Wait just a minute baby girl. Let me get everything out of it and then you can play in it if you want," I said while taking out the food and toys.

Anna checked the whole outside of the carrier. I think she smelled every inch of it by the time I had taken everything out of it. I left the door open so she could check out the padded bed inside of it.

"It looks like she likes it Rita," Jack said with a chuckle. "Will you be getting off work early tomorrow?" he asked

"I think I could do that. What do you have in mind?" I asked.

"You will be leaving for San Francisco in about two weeks and I would like as much time with you as I can get before you leave," he said giving me a smile.

"Yes, I think I can manage to get off early most every day while I am painting. Do you want to meet me at the Rooster each day," I asked.

"That sounds like a good deal," he said looking at the clock. "I need to go catch the bus so I can get home tonight," he added getting up and heading for the front door.

"Good night, I said meeting him at the door for a few kisses and a couple of great hugs.

"See you tomorrow," he said with a wave as he went down the steps to catch the bus.

"Tell me what happened today at work," Nell requested as I closed the door.

I started at the beginning and told her all that had happen. Then I showed her the picture and told her of the changes he wanted me to make.

"Do you think you can do all of that the way he wants it done. I mean isn't it a little different painting the size of this one and painting a life-size mural?" she asked.

"Oh I am sure there will be a lot of differences, but I think I can do it. Besides everyone will get to see it that comes into the café, and I plan to sign my name somewhere on it," I said laughing.

"Well we had better get in bed soon or you may be too tired to start on that mural tomorrow," Nell said with a yawn.

"True," I said looking around for Anna.

Then I remember that the last time I saw her she was snooping around the new carrier. As I walked into the kitchen she peeked out from inside the carrier at me.

"It's time for bed baby girl. Are you coming or are you sleeping in there?" I asked.

"Meow" came her answer as she ran past me to the bedroom and jumped onto the bed.

Sleep came quick, but morning seemed even faster. When I opened my eyes I didn't see Anna, so I got dressed quickly thinking that maybe Nell got up early and Anna heard her. If so then Anna would be in the kitchen looking for food.

Nell wasn't up yet but Anna had found one of the toys I had left on the table last night.

"I see you picked out one of the toys to try first," I said gathering up the rest of them.

I put them in a plastic bag and closed it then snapped it into a side pocket of the carrier.

It didn't take long for her to notice that I had the refrigerator door open. She sat herself down on the side that had her food and meowed then went to the side that had the milk and meowed again.

"Oh you must be a hungry girl today since you are asking for both right off," I said laughing. "Ok, give me a chance to get a few other things out of the frig first. Go sit next to your dish," I added.

She trotted over and sat there waiting for a few minutes before starting to play with her new toy that was close by.

"Good morning Rita," Nell said poking her head around the edge of the door.

"Meow," Anna said.

"And good morning to you too," Nell said returning to peek around the edge of the door.

"Good morning Nell," I said quickly before she disappeared again. "I figured scrambled eggs and toast this morning. Is that ok with you?" I asked raising my voice for Nell to hear me.

"Sounds good!" Nell yelled from the bathroom while putting on her makeup.

"I'm sure glad I haven't gotten in the habit of doing that each morning," I said in a low voice to Anna as I put her food in her dishes.

"Meow," Anna said as if to agree.

"Breakfast is ready and it looks like we get to race to the bus again this morning," I said laughing. "The clock is ticking its count down.

"I'm hurrying," Nell said rushing and sitting down, "Yep, it's time to run," Nell said looking at the clock as she took the last swallow of her coffee.

"I was already at the door with my jacket, as Anna came to say good-bye when Nell came down the hall.

I opened the door as she grabbed her keys from the hook.

"Here we come George," I said and we hurried down the steps and ran to the bus stop.

"We got here first today George," I said handing him my pass.

"Maybe, but not by much," he said with a chuckle while Nell dropped her token in the farebox. We hurried and sat down as George started driving.

It didn't take long before I was walking into the Rooster.

"Hi Rita, come to my office," Charlie said as he walked that direction with a cup of coffee.

I just smiled at Sandy as I walked past her. She was holding up her hand as if to ask what was happening.

"Hi Charlie," I said as I walked into his office, "What's up?" I asked.

"Well since you are going to be painting I thought we had better figure out how much paint you are going to need. And what I should pay you for doing it," he said.

"I'm not sure how much paint it's going to take, but I will stay as long as it takes to get it painted. I redrew the picture you wanted and made the changes you talked about. I brought it with me this morning," I informed him. "We are talking about making it all life-size. Right?" I added

"Yes. Where is the picture? Can I see it?" he asked.

"Yes. But before we set any prices or costs, I would like to go to the art shop and talk to Lucinda. She can give me a better idea about the cost of the paints and their drying time." I said.

"Ok, but at least let me see what you drew up last night," he said getting more excited by the second.

"Ok," I said as I laid the picture on his desk.

"Oh yes, this is just what I was talking about. Go see Lucinda as soon as possible and let me know what she says," he said holding up the picture as if to place it on his office wall.

Then he placed the picture on his desk and started to write something on a piece of his office stationary, then he stamped it. "Take this with you and see if you can keep the price as low as you can," he said handing me the paper. "This is great," he said holding up the picture again with a big smile.

"Well, don't just stand there you have work to do. Go find out what you need and get started on it," he said almost laughing.

I told Sandy on my way out the door that I was going after paint and left her standing there with questions.

I had to hurry to catch George so I could get to Blane St.

"Hi George, I'm heading for Blane St

for paint," I said as I got on the bus.

"Do you remember your way from Slone St" he asked.

"Yeah, I'm pretty sure I remember where it is. But remind me where to get off just in case," I said sitting down across from him.

"Ok, here you are," George said laughing.

"Oh thanks, I guess I was daydreaming a little as I watched the streets fly by. Slone St sure seemed to come up fast," I said laughing. "Later," I add as I got off.

Soon I was standing in front of "Magical Arts for the Artist", Lucinda's shop.

Chapter Thirteen

I opened the door and spotted Lucinda at the back of the shop. "Hi Lucinda," I shouted.

"Oh Miss Anna," your back for more paints?" she asked starting to walk towards me.

"I'm not Anna, I'm Rita," I said as she got closer.

"Oh, so you are. Twins always mix me up," she laughed. "What can I help you with?" she asked.

It took a little while but I explained the job I had been asked to create and all of the colors that were needed. While she took out her pencil and pad and wrote it all down. Then came the time to go around and price all of the paint that was going to be needed.

All together and as close as we could figure it was going to cost Charlie around five hundred dollars just for the supplies and paint. Then I asked her, "If you were to paint a life-size picture like this, what would you charge for doing it?"

"Well that is a tough one but I don't think I would do it for any less than one thousand. But again you are new at doing anything this large so I would say ask him to pay you at least eight hundred. Are you as good as your sister?" she asked.

"Not yet but I am getting there. I haven't learned to do the two pictures in one. But I am pretty good and landscapes and perspective drawings," I boasted.

"Oh Charlie gave me this to give to you," I said handing her the paper he had written out to her.

"Oh yes, this will work. We have the list of all that you will need that I can send you back to him with along with two gallons of base coat you will need so you can start on an even color. Map out the area you will be painting on and tape it off and paint inside that area. This will become like your canvas," she explained. "Here you go, the two gallons and the brush, tape, and roller you will need to start. I can bring everything else over early tomorrow morning. Say about eight AM," she informed me handing the list of items and information to give to Charlie.

I folded the paper and put it in my jacket pocket, then gathered up the paint and the sack with the brushes and tape. I nodded to her and said good-by as I raced back to catch George.

As I got on the bus I place the gallons and sack on the seat up front then stepped back to pay George.

"Painting?" George asked.

"Yes, my first art piece I have been commissioned to do," I bragged in a low voice so no one else could hear.

"Where is it going to hang. At the Rooster?" he asked.

"Now where else would I be painting?" I asked with a chuckle before sitting down.

"Well, I'll be watching you," he said laughing.

It didn't take long before I was putting the gallons and sack on the counter as I walked back to Charlie's office.

"Here is the paper from Lucinda with all of the cost. You need to call her and tell her it is ok before I start using the paint she sent me back with," I said.

"Ok, I'll do that right now so you can get started," he said picking up the phone and motioning for me to leave the office.

I grabbed the tape measure off his desk with him giving me a nod and started for the far wall of the rooster.

I measured one foot from the right corner and made sure it was the same distance from the floor to the ceiling. Then I measured one and a half feet down from the ceiling. Now I just needed to find out how wide Charlie wanted the room to be. I taped off the area I had just measured and waited for Charlie to come out of his room. I sat down and stirred the first gallon of paint for a good ten minutes, then decided to go ask.

As I walked through the open door of his office he looked to be reading the newspaper.

"Charlie, how wide do you want that painting to be?" I asked.

He didn't move except for one finger on his left hand.

I walked around to get a better view and I could see that his eyes looked strange.

"JIMMY HELP!"

Jimmy came running. He was a medic in the army.

He came in and took a quick look and call 911. The ambulance came and picked up Charlie and the doctor later said we had gotten help just in time. He had had a minor stroke. But he would be ok. Betty and Fred stayed at the Rooster and kept business going.

I went back to the Rooster and used my own judgment on the width of the picture. I finished taping off the area that was to be my canvas and started painting.

Jack came by work and I went him with him for a few hours before going back to Nell's house. I needed to just relax after all it had been quite a day, full of excitement and trauma all at the same time.

As Jack and I got back to Nell's house I opened the screen door and was ready to put the key in the lock when Nell opened it. Standing beside her was Anna. Both greeted us at the same time. Jack came in for a few minutes and got a cup of coffee while I told

Nell everything that had happened.

"Wow. Do the doctors know what caused the problem? I mean Charlie isn't that old," she asked.

"No, but I guess he will be ok," I said thinking about my future self's reaction.

"Why do you say that?" she asked.

"Well, Anna didn't seem surprised to see him when she came by to visit," I answered.

"True," Nell said with a chuckle. "Ok, then I won't worry about him then. I'll just ask the pastor to pray," she said while walking back toward her bedroom.

"Well, I need to get to the bus stop so I can get home tonight," Jack announced. "Bye Nell," he yelled as I walked him to the door.

After a few kisses,, he took off in a mad run to catch the bus.

When I got to work, Sandy let me know that Lucinda had dropped off all of the paints and supplies I was going to need. Jimmy had piled them all in the corner for me.

"Right on. Thank, Sandy, THANKS JIMMY," I yelled.

This time of the morning the only customer at the The Rooster Café were the ones used to us being loud and having fun.

"Hey Rita," Bill said giving a tug on my apron as I walked by.

"Yes," I answered.

"What are you doing over there?" he asked pointing at the area I had taped off.

"I'm building a new room," I said with a chuckle.

"Is Charlie expanding?" he asked.

"No, it's just that we have a painting that changes over there. And Charlie figured we needed something else on this side of the Rooster for balance," I shared.

"Oooh," Bill trailed off into thought.

I worked on completing the canvas part of the painting and then decided to get a soda.

"Any word of how Charlie is doing?" I asked Sandy. "Jimmy called the hospital earlier and they want to keep him for another day or two, to make sure everything is ok. But they said he is doing good. They want to run a few more tests," she added.

"That's good. I called last night but they couldn't tell me anything yet," I said.

"Jimmy plans to go see him after work today," she informed me.

"Well, I had better get back to work on this painting he wants. Maybe I can have a lot of it finished before he gets back," I said with a smile.

I went right to work measuring the height again so I could figure the best width to make the painting. Then I taped that side and finished painting the base coat.

At this point, the wall looked like a giant artist canvas.

'Now to get the right angles set to make the picture look as if you could walk into the next room.' I thought.

I turned and studied the rest of the café. Because I knew if the line of sight was set wrong it wouldn't look right. With a regular size painting, one could just hang it at a different level to make it look different. This was going to be set so the angles had to be just right to keep the illusion alive.

I used an off white chalk to make my guidelines with. Then framed the back wall of the illusionary room I was making. Then I needed to put in temporary lines for the floor tile. And I didn't want to forget the furniture placements.

'Ok, I think I have things pretty well under control and I need a break.' I thought taking a deep breath.

"The phone rang just as I sat down at the counter. Sandy answered the phone. I couldn't hear much of the conversation. Then she said "Ok" and hung up.

"Who was that?" I asked.

"That was Brenda, Charlie's new wife. She said she would be coming in to help out until Charlie got on his feet again," Sandy explained while Jimmy and Fred were both and the ordering window.

"I didn't know he had gotten married again," Fred said.

"I didn't either, that's news to me," Jimmy agreed.

"Did you know that Charlie got married?" I asked Sandy.

"Nope hadn't heard a word," she said looking at all of us.

Betty, walked in just as Sandy served me a soda.

"Betty did you know that Charlie got married again?" Sandy asked.

"Yeah that was last week if I remember right," she said. "Why?" she asked.

"She plans to come in and take care of the café while Charlie gets better," I said informing her of the call.

"Well there really isn't that much to take care of except maybe the ordering of supplies and we just add them to the list in his office as we run low," she said and we all gave a big smile in agreement.

"True, but I guess she can sit in the office like Charlie does," I said with a chuckle.

We all started laughing as if to release tension from a stranger coming in and taking Charlie's place. After all none of us had ever met her as far as we knew.

Just then a tall slender woman walked through the café door. Betty went to greet her. But instead of her sitting down at a table or at the bar they walked towards all of us.

Things had been slow for a few hours and we had all taken a break together.

"This is Brenda, Charlie's wife," Betty said with an open hand towards Brenda.

"Glad to meet you," we all said pretty much in unison.

"I can tell you are all quite a team, as you did answer together," she said. "Would you like to show me around?" she asked looking at Betty.

"Sure not a problem," Betty said as they both strolled off towards the back toward Charlie's office.

I finished my drink and got back to work on the painting. Jimmy and Fred went back to work getting things set up for dinner.

It wasn't long before Betty came back to the front.

I looked up after putting my brushed in a bucket and motioned for Betty to come over where I was.

"What did you find out about her?" I sort of whispered.

"She has known Charlie for about eight years. She has been his private bookkeeper and tax person for the last three. And they got engaged two years ago and got married a week ago," she said smiling.

"Good then she knows the café from the other side," I said with a smile. "Was there any news about Charlie?" I added

"He should be getting home tomorrow according to his doctor," she said. "But bed rest for the next two weeks at least," she added.

"Well maybe she can let him come to the Rooster long enough to see the finished painting on the wall, I hope," I said looking back at the wall.

"It looks real good so far. It's as if you have added another room," Betty said pointing at the decoration of the back wall of the room I was painting.

"That's the idea," I said laughing.

"Well I have customers that just came in," she said with a chuckle while walking towards the door.

I looked a little closer at the painting and noticed I had a few things I needed to touch up.

"Ah, there, that's better," I said under my breath. 'There, it's all finished,' I thought to myself as I stepped back to get a better look at it. 'Now the only thing to do is to move the tables and chairs back into their places and take down the drop cloth,' I thought.

Jimmy and Fred had helped me hang it just far enough from the wall for me to work without anyone else seeing what I was doing. It was to be a surprise to everyone when it was done.

But most of my workmates and friends knew what I was doing. So it would just be a surprise to the customers.

I walked back to ask Fred and Jimmy to help me take down the drop cloth.

Brenda followed them and me back to the front. She wanted to know what we were up to.

Fred grabbed the ladder on the way. And Jimmy grabbed a long pole we have for putting up decorations.

"Ready Fred," Jimmy said holding one side of the drop cloth.

"Yep, he goes," Fred said as he

unhooked his side. "Du Dah!" he said as the cloth fell at our feet.

"Wow! That is wonderful. It is as if we have added another room to the café," Brenda almost shouted in surprise.

"Good I was hoping for that effect," I said laughing.

"I think we all agree. You have talent like your sister. I bet one of these dayss you will be able to paint pictures like hers," Betty said.

"I totally agree," Jimmy almost shouted.

It caught the attention of the few customers that were sitting towards the front of the Rooster and they started to clap.

"We didn't know you were expanding the Rooster," one of them said.

"Oh we didn't expand the Rooster," Betty said with a chuckle.

"But you added another room," another said.

"No, Come take a closer look," I said motioning for them to come take a look.

"Oh, Oh my. It's a wall painting. But it looks so real," one said.

"That's the idea," chuckled Jimmy on his way back to the kitchen with Fred following him grabbing the other end of the drop cloth.

Betty and I started taking down the ladder.

"Leave it there. I'm coming back for it," Fred shouted.

"Do you think Charlie will feel well enough to come in and see the wall since it is finished?" I asked directing my question to Brenda.

"I will be talking to him later tonight and I can ask. I'm sure he will want to see it as soon as he is able," she said smiling while looking closely at the painting. "You did sign this work of art didn't you," she asked looking back at me.

"Yes I signed my name to the picture in the painting, so it wouldn't be so obvious," I answered pointing to the picture.

"Can you again sign your initials at least in the right corner in the orange?" she requested pointing at the area.

"Sure, that's not a problem," I said taking the smallest brush out of the bucket and dipping it in the black paint.

"Is that what you were wanting?" I asked Looking over at Brenda, who had been watching me the whole time.

"Perfect," she said with a large smile. "I love this whole idea. Charlie told me about your sister coming and visiting the painting of hers he had bought. You two are quite talented," she added.

"Thank you," I said giving a slight bow before laughing. "I think we just found something that we liked doing," I added.

Fred came back and got the ladder as I turned around to face the door and Jack walked in at the same time.

"Wow now that is what I would call a great add-on," he said with a chuckle. "Are you ready to go?" he added looking at me.

"Before you leave I need to know if you are Charlie talked about you getting paid for doing all of this?" Brenda interrupted.

"Well yes," I answered shyly, worried that Brenda would think that he was paying me too much.

"What did he offer to pay you?" she asked point-blank.

"Eight hundred plus the paint," I offered.

"No! Not happening!" she said putting her hand on her hips and looking straight at me. "This is worth a good sixteen hundred is one cent. And I will make sure you have a check for that amount in the morning," she said. "You are that good and don't let anyone tell you differently," she said giving me a hug. "Go have fun," she added nearly pushing me towards the door.

"That art wall you did was the best. It looked like the Rooster actually added another room to the café," Jack said as we walked out the door. "And you're getting paid sixteen hundred dollars for doing it. Wow." He added. "Who was that woman?'

"Oh that is Brenda, Charlie's wife/bookkeeper/tax person," I said with a smile.

"I didn't know he was married," Jack said being surprised.

"That's ok. None of us knew either until today," I said laughing. "Anyway, Charlie should be out of the hospital and back home soon. But Brenda is taking care of the business until Charlie is able to come back," I informed him.

"Well that's cool that he has someone to take his place that knows what is going on," he said. "So what do you want to do this evening?" he asked taking my hand.

"I don't know let me think about it for a few minutes," I said as we joined in laughter.

"You know, I feel like a movie. Or maybe a couple of movies," I said looking over at Jack with a big smile. "After all, I have the money I need now to make the trip to San Francisco and still have some saved for a visit back here after a couple of months if things don't work out there," I added.

"Ok, what movies did you have in mind and where are they playing?" he asked with a gentle squeeze of my hand.

"Oh. Maybe Jack Theater? I hear the popcorn is fresh and the seats are comfortable," I said with a giggle.

"You're on. What's playing there tonight?"

"I'm not sure. I think there was an action and something funny," I said looking over at him and laughing.

"Well then I guess we will have to check it out," he said as we got on the bus.

Chapter Fourteen

It didn't take long before we were at Jack's apartment and had the popcorn popped and had just sat down when Max came running in and jump onto the couch with us. Then he tried to sit on our laps.

"Max! Get over here and set. You have the whole end of the couch to sit on," Jack said laughing. "I will give you some popcorn but not too, much so eat it slowly."

"I didn't know that Max liked popcorn," I said looking over at Max as he buried his face in the bowl.

"He thinks he is a human," Jack laughed. "I treat him as if he is most of the time," Jack added.

"The movie is starting," I said snuggling up to Jack. I curled up on the couch and pulled a blanket over my feet.

The movies were fun, but I guess I was more tired than I thought. The next thing I knew, the sun was coming through Jack's window and I was waking up on the couch with a pillow under my head and covered with a cozy soft blanket.

"Good morning love. Did you sleep ok?" Jack asked as he came from the kitchen.

"I must have really been tired," I said with a smile.

"I have breakfast ready if you don't mind cereal and bacon. Max and I keep it simple around here," he said laughing.

"That sounds good. But I need to call the café first," I said

"Sure the phone is over there," he said pointing to the corner.

"Hello Sandy, is Brenda or Charlie there yet?" I asked.

"Brenda is here. Hold on a minute," she said putting the phone down.

"Hello this is Brenda," she said.

"Hi Brenda, this is Rita. Have you talked to Charlie yet?" I asked.

"Yes, he will be here at 2:30 today to look at your painting. I think that would be a good time for you to be here so we can get you paid. I heard you plan to go to San Francisco to learn painting," she said.

"Yes, my sister told me about her teacher and I want to be able to paint like here someday," I said with a slight giggle.

"Well you come by then and I am sure we can get you the money. See you then. Bye," she said just as she hung up the phone.

"It's all set, I get paid today for the wall mural. I'm pretty much packed and my rent is already paid in San Francisco. So I can leave tomorrow morning," I informed Jack.

"So the adventure begins AA?" he said with a big smile.

Time seemed to fly by and it was soon time to catch the buses so we could meet up with Brenda and Charlie at The Rooster Café.

When I walked in I was surprised. The place was decorated as if for a party and the drop cloth was covering the painting again.

"What is going on?" I asked Sandy looking over the counter at her.

"Well it is sort of a surprise revealing/going away party," she said.

"Are you saying that Charlie hasn't seen the painting yet?" I asked.

"Nope, Brenda went to get him and gave us this idea before she left," she informed me.

"Well I have to say this is pretty nice," Jack said putting his arms around me and giving me a hug.

"I think so too," Fred said holding up a large cake and laughing.

"Well this is turning out to be a great day so far," I said.

Just then Brenda and Charlie walked through the door.

Charlie looked around and said, "What the heck are all of you up to now?"

Fred spoke out loud and clear so everyone could hear," It is a welcome back/revealing/going away party," then gave a hearty laugh.

Which everyone joined.

"A what kind of party?" Charlie

questioned.

"It's a welcome back glad to see you party for you. An unveiling party for the wall, and a going-away party for Rita, all in one," Brenda explained.

"Oh! Well then let's get it going. Pass out the cake and drinks," Charlie said laughing and moved closer to the wall.

"Maybe stand in the middle of the room dear," Brenda suggested to Charlie.

"Ok, I think I am ready. Takedown the drop cloth," he said.

And as it dropped I heard him take a deep breath.

"Oh my gosh! It is so much better than I could have dreamed. It looks like we added a new room to The Rooster," he said.

And with that everyone in the café clapped and cheered.

Brenda leaned towards me and handed me the check and said, "Thank you for such a great painting."

"This is really nice and worth every penny. I now have two paintings from the famous Stolks sisters," Charlie announced proudly.

I smiled and took a deep bow. And as I stood back up Jack grabbed me in his arms, lifting me slightly and we spun around in laughter.

"So how soon are you leaving for San Francisco?" Charlie asked.

"Well, I have everything pretty much packed and I was thinking about catching the bus in a couple of days," I explained.

"You will call once in a while and let us all know what is happening right?" Sandy asked almost pleading.

"Of course you are all family. I have already paid my rent on a place there. I can get mail at the place I am renting. I will send you a postcard when I get moved in," I explained.

The party went well and the customers that were there at the time seemed to enjoy themselves.

Jack took me back to Nell's after the party and stayed long enough to eat dinner with us.

The next few days went fast. I got up early Wednesday morning and put my bus ticket in the jacket pocket.

Jack called, "Don't call and taxi or plan to take the bus to the station. Are you all packed and ready to go?" he asked.

"Yes all packed and I was just getting ready to call you. Are you going to meet me at the bus station?" I asked.

"No, I am coming to get you," he stated. "So wait for me," he added.

"Ok I will wait until you get here to put Anna in the carrier," I explained.

"Okay, see you soon," he said the hung up.

"Nell had just left for work after a tearful goodbye and handing me a stack of pre-stamped postcards with orders to write every week.

"Well Anna, are you ready for a new way to travel. I have toys you haven't see yet," I said with a giggle while I sat down and pet her. Everything O was taking was already in the hallway.

Soon the doorbell rang. "That must be Jack. Are you ready to go on a trip, Anna?" I asked as I went to answer the door with Anna on my heels.

"Hi Jack," I said looking past him while opening the door. He gave me a kiss as he came through the door.

"Are all of these going with you?" he asked while picking up the largest one.

I glanced over his shoulder as he carried my largest suitcase down the front stairs and saw he was carrying it towards a chauffeured car. I carried the two smaller bags to the car after placing Anna in her carrier.

"You rented a special car for me to go to the bus station?" I asked.

"Well, sort of. It is in my contract that I can have use of a chauffeured car four times a year," he said laughing.

Then he turned and walked up the stairs with me. He took Anna to the car while I locked up Nell's house.

After almost an hour's ride with lots of hugs and kisses, we arrived at the bus station.

Jack looked at his watch. "We got here in plenty of time. We have an hour before your bus pulls in. Are you hungry? There is a little place around the corner that has pretty good food. Well, better than the bus station," he said in laughter.

"Let's check me in first. I think that most of my luggage needs to go in the bus's cargo hold," I suggested.

"Oh yes very true," he said while moving all of my luggage closer to the weight station.

I was next in line and it wasn't long before we were next door ordering a couple of sandwiches to go and a quick meal to be eaten while waiting on the bus to come in.

I took the last bite of mine and Jack looked at his watch. "It is about time to get over to the station and make sure you don't miss your bus. I miss you already," he said with a slightly sad smile.

"I feel the same way but you know I have to go take care of this part of my life. I promise to write real often and call once I get a phone," I said trying to brighten his smile while feeling the same way. "I love you a lot and that won't change. You know that," I added while walking around the corner to the station.

"I know, I love you very much too. We need to work on setting a wedding date," he added smiling through almost teary eyes.

"I agree," I said hearing my voice almost cracking as I reach form another long hug as my bus drove in.

I watch as they loaded my luggage onto the bus with Jack standing with his arms around me and Anna sitting in he carried at my feet.

"You still have on the promise ring, right?" he asked as the bus door opened for passengers.

"Yes and around my neck is where I keep it. Unless I am taking a bath or swimming because I don't want to lose it," I explained.

"Good, but when you go swimming, make sure you lock it up. Okay?" he requested.

"You know I will," I said just as the driver called for everyone to get on the bus.

"Bye, I love you," I said "And I will call as soon as I get a phone,"

He grabbed one last hug before I picked up Anna and got on the bus.

I managed to sit next to a window and waved as the bus pulled out of the station.

"Well Anna we are on our way to California," I said while putting her carrier on my lap.

The carrier was tall enough that she could stand up in it to stretch. I looked through the mesh screen at her and she was looking out the window, seemingly to be transfixed on all of the movement outside.

The sandwiched and two drinks were in my backpack at my feet along with her toys and food packets.

I took a long deep breath feeling that everything was under control, so I could relax a little.

We made a lot of stops along the way, letting off some passengers while picking up more.

After a while, the days and nights almost blended together. I managed to get a few quick meals along the way.

The closer I got to California we seemed to collect stranger people. I got up at one point to walk to the bathroom and when I got back the person that had been sitting next to me moved all of my things including Anna's carrier to the aisle seat.

I didn't want to start anything so I sat down in the seat hoping that they would be getting off soon. Meanwhile, Anna didn't have the window to keep her entertained and she started to meow.

The person next to me told me to keep her quiet. She was disturbing their sleep. I told them she was wanted her window back as politely as I could.

It was about another two hours before they got off the bus to get something from one of the stops. While they were gone Anna and I took back out window seat.

They didn't get back on the bus so we had both seats for a few hundred miles. I felt I could really finally relax.

Soon we stopped in a small town and a young girl, I'd say maybe ten years old and her father got on. I moved back to the window seat so she could sit down and her father sat right across from her. She spotted Anna right off and played with her for the longest time by moving the string that held the toy that hung from the top of her carried.

They both got off in the next town and this small lady got on and sat down beside me. She looked to be old enough to be a grandmother or maybe a great grandmother. She sat quietly for a while and took a short nap. Then when she woke up she opened this large cloth bag she has and took out some yarn and a couple of knitting needle and started knitting.

After she had been knitting for a few hours, it started to look like it may turn out to be a hat. She spotted my watching.

"Do you know how to knit?" she asked looking kindly at me.

"No, it looks complicated," I answered.

"It's not really. There are two basic stitched," she offered. "Do you mind?" she asked reaching toward my head with the half-finished hat in her hands.

"Well, no I guess," I said bowing my head toward her.

"Oh perfect. My judgment is still good," she said with a beaming smile. "I take this trip once a month and I make a hat for the person next to me each time," she explained with a small chuckle.

She had just handed me the hat as we pulled into the bus station.

"Well, it's been nice dearie. Enjoy your new hat. This is where I get off. My daughter lives here and should be picking me up in about ten minutes," she said with a wave as she got up and walked down the aisle to the door.

"Wow Anna, look at me. I have a new hat," I said putting the hat on. I fit perfectly. Anna tilted her head and gave a long "Meow."

The seat next to me remained empty for the rest of the night and till midafternoon the next day. The quiet time gave me time to draw and sleep without worry.

There were a number of empty seats closer to the front of the bus so even when passengers started to get on the bus, they filled the seats closer to the front. I had another night of peace.

Then early in the morning, we stopped at once of the larger bus station that had a great café hooked to it and we had a few hours to wait. I put on my backpack and grabber Anna's carrier and took advantage of letting her out on a leash for a longer time than she had been having at other stops.

I grabbed a couple more sandwiches to go and a few more drinks before getting back on the bus.

I got back on just in time and managed to claim the window seat just in time because the very next person that got on sat down right beside me.

I looked up from placing my backpack on the floor between my foot and the bus wall. There was what I would describe as a middle-aged man with a suit jacket with a vest under it. He looked down the aisle as the bus started down the road and stroked his goatee. That was a little strange to me. But he managed to catch the attention of young boy sitting in from of me and it wasn't too long before the tow children in the seats ahead of me were leaning over the seats watching his every move.

You see, he turned out to be a magician and we were all entertained for with tricks, jokes, and conversation for the next twelve hours.

My eyes started to close and Anna had already gone to sleep with a full belly. I think I got a few hours of sleep before I was woken up by the very loud almost grumbling sound.

Anna meowed softly. I opened my eyes to see what was going on.

"Shhhh Anna, Not too loud. He's okay he's just asleep," I explained quietly.

She tilted her head and laid down again. I put on my headphones with the music just loud enough to blend in with the magician's snoring.

The magician got off the bus in Los Angeles. So I knew it wouldn't be long before I would be in San Francisco.

I had an empty seat next to me once again until we got within that last thirty miles of San Francisco and the bus fill up and a few people standing in the aisle.

I took out my sketch pad and started sketching what I saw. Then someone noticed.

Chapter Fifteen

As I was sketching I was listening to some of the conversations of the group that had gotten on at the last stop. They were all part of an actors guild headed for a play in San Francisco.

As I finished the sketch I noticed that one person was sort of looking over my shoulder. He was standing slightly back but beside my seat.

"I don't mean to bother you, but I noticed that you are great at details in your sketch. I mean we are all together as a group and you have drawn the picture as if you had seen if from the back of the bus. I'm even in it," he said sounding surprised. "How did you do that?" he asked.

"Well, after everyone was on, I had to work my way from the back of the bus to my seat. And I have a pretty good memory. So I drew what I remembered seeing," I explained.

"Can I see the sketch for a minute?" he asked holding out his hand.

I reluctantly handed him my sketch pad. "Okay but please be careful with it," I said.

"Oh yes mam by all means," he said as he took it.

"Hey, guys look at this. Look what I'm holding," He said holding up the sketch for all of them to see.

One of the young ladies got all excited, "Is there a way we can buy it from you? It would make a great present to our director," she stated.

"Well, I don't know," I said thoughtfully.

Then I noticed they were all looking through their pockets and handing what they had to the guy standing next to me.

"We have three hundred and ten dollars. Would that be enough?" he asked with a large smile.

I looked up at him smiled and reached into my backpack to get my camera. "First let me take a picture of it so I can remember my trip," I said with a slight chuckle.

"Oh and please sign and date it for us," he requested.

"Oh yes of course," I said taking it back, signed and dated it then took a couple of pictures of it just in case the first one didn't turn out.

A few minutes later we were pulling into the San Francisco bus station.

"Anna we are very lucky today. We got to San Francisco just at the right time.

That means we can be in our new place tonight.

I put on my backpack and took Anna's carrier off the bus and went to the nearest phone and call Ms. Beca March.

"Hello Ms. Beca," Yes she said

"Rita here. I just got off the bus," I said. I can be there as soon as I can get a taxi," I added.

"Ok, see you then. I'm in Apt A," she replied.

As I hung up the phone I looked through the window and there was a taxi sitting near the station. I gathered up my large suitcase and placed Anna's carrier on top. I was glad that the large case had wheels. I managed to get to the taxi and he helped load everything into the taxi.

"Where to miss?" he asked as he got back into the car.

"228 Lauren Street please," I said

"Yes mam, right away," he said starting the car.

"Are there very many art studios in San Francisco?" I asked.

"There are a few strewn throughout the city. Are you an artist?" he asked.

"Yes, I am here looking for my teacher, but I don't have an address for him," I answered quickly while watching for anything that looked like it may be Master Bastrono studio.

"Here you are, miss. That will be $8.35," he said stopping the car and opening his door.

He went to the back and took my suitcase out and sat it on the sidewalk and then stood there with his hand out.

I paid him and he drove away leaving me there to figure out how to get everything inside the apartment house by myself.

So I proceeded to put Anna's carrier on the steps then got my larger suitcase up two steps past Anna. The repeated this with Anna's carrier until I had everything inside and safe.

I found apartment A close to the front door and knocked on the door.

"Beca March?" I asked as the door opened just enough to see that someone was there.

"Yes?" came the answer in a questioning tone.

"I'm Rita, I called earlier. I just got off the bus and took a taxi here. Can I get the key from you for the apartment I rented from you?" I asked.

She opened the door far enough that I could get a good look at her. She was a little older than middle age. Her salt and pepper hair was slicked back in a bun. She looked up at me over her small framed reading glasses and gave me a big smile while reaching into the pocket of her apron for the key.

"Here you are, dear. Please come down and visit with me when you get this settled. I can tell you the best places to buy things and get the best deals," she said handing me the key. "Yours is the roof apartment, I think you will like it. Go to the third floor and then take the stairs in the right corner," she added.

"Then she looked past me and seen my luggage. "Let me get you some help. My grandson is visiting today," she said looking back into her apartment. "Johnny, I need your help please," she yelled.

"This is my grandson Johnny," she said as the strong-looking young man maybe in his early twenties, dressed in khaki pants and a green tank top walked up behind her.

"Rita needs some help getting her things to the roof apartment," she told him.

"Glad to help," he said with a big smile as he walked past her and picked up Anna's carried and my large suitcase. Then he stood there waiting for me to lead the way.

"Thank you," I said turning toward Beca.

On our way up the stairs, Johnny asked where I was from and what I hoped to do in Frisco as he called San Francisco. What my cats name was and how old I was and what kind of work was I looking for.

I answered most of his questions with the smallest amount of information possible. I guess I was feeling a little uneasy with all of the questions. I was raised that if the person asked too many personal questions the first time you meet them it could be dangerous.

"Those stairs lead to your apartment. I

think you will like it. It is larger than most of the apartments here. Grandma lets it go for less money because it is out of the way and a lot of stairs," he laughed.

I opened the door and had to take a deep breath. I was larger in a way I hadn't imagined.

"This is nice. I like it. I am sure Anna and I will be ok here. Thank you for carrying my things up for me," I said reaching out to shake hands.

He shook my hand and gave a slight bow with a large smile and left.

I closed the door and took Anna out of her carrier, put on her leash and I opened the small back door that I am sure was a large window at one time. We stepped out onto the roof and took a look around,

I could see a few trees scattered around between the house, but not many. The houses here seemed to be stacked together almost as close as the ones in New York.

We went back inside and I made sure the back door was closed and locked before taking off the leash and harness and let Anna check out our new home. I opened my suitcase and changed into something more relaxing. Then I sat on the floor and made a list of all the things I needed to make this our new home, while Anna curled up on the floor in the close I just took off.

"Oh Anna, this is our new home. You will see, I think you will like it once we get a couch and a bed," I said laughing while giving her a few strokes. "Now let me see. I need food, shelf paper, paper plates, a couch, abed," I said out loud while writing them on my list. "Maybe we can get a TV tomorrow," I added.

"With that Anna said "Meow," In agreement.

"Well, I best get going if I plan to get all of this before the stores close," I said, petting Anna a few more stokes. "Now you be a good girl while I am gone," I said while placing her food and water in her bowls not too far from where she was laying. Then I walked out the door making sure it was locked behind me.

I went down to see Beca and find out what all was close by. Maybe I would have to go far for the things I needed for the night.

She was very helpful. She told me about Grosemen's Department Store about four blocks away. And Belder's Groceries was in the next block over. And there was Dale's Café just up the street a few blocks and they were needing help the last time she was there. That was a possible job.

I managed to get everything on my list and the best part of all, they were willing to deliver all of the things I bought from them. I had just enough time to go to Dale's Café, get me and Anna's dinner and get back to the apartment in time for all of the deliveries.

"Hi Anna, I'm home with dinner," I said as I walked through the door.

"She looked up from a resting position and gave a happy meow, got up and stretched real big.

I sat there on the floor and shared my dinner with my best friend in San Francisco. While we ate I was looking around the room to figure out where we wanted the bed and couch.

The apartment was like one very large room with a kitchen area at one end and a full bathroom at the other end.

"Oh my goodness, I almost forgot but I bet you didn't. I brought you a box and litter. Here you go baby girl," I said placing the box on the floor in one corner.

She gave me a happy meow and ran to the box.

Just then there was a knock on the door. I opened the door and two men were standing there holding the box springs and mattress.

"Where do you want us to put your bed," asked the taller of the two.

"On that end of the room, please," I said pointing.

"The couch is downstairs and we will bring it up next," the shorter one said.

They set up my bed while I stood to one side and held Anna. Then they brought up the couch and I had them place it right in the middle of the room.

"Thank you for helping me out by placing these items where I needed them," I said as they left the second time.

I closed the door and Anna and I sat down on the couch and took a few long deep breaths.

I put Anna's blanket on the couch and after she fussed around with it for a few minutes she settled down and fell asleep.

I had just sat down and relaxed with a book that I had brought with me when there was a knock at the door. I placed the book gently on the couch and went to the door.

"Who is it?" I asked before opening the door.

"It's Bobby from Belder's Groceries with your order," came the voice on the other side of the door.

"Okay, just a minute," I said as I unlocked the door. There in front of me stood young man maybe in his late teens holding two medium size boxes.

"Where would you like me to put your order?" he said standing at the door with his arms full.

"Thank you, just place them on the counter, please," I said pointing in the direction of the kitchen with a smile as I shut the door.

"Yes mam, and thank you. He said as he carried everything to the kitchen. "Oh yes, my boss said to tell you, that you can call the store and we can fill your order and then you can pay me when I deliver it," he added as he turns to face me with a big smile.

"Thank you. That is good to know. Here put this in your pocket," I said handing him a dollar. "I know that isn't a lot but that is what I have handy," I added with a smile.

"So have you worked for Belder's long?" I asked.

"Just since the eleventh grade, a couple of years," he replied.

"How is the neighborhood here?" I inquired.

"Well, for the most part, it is pretty quiet and safe," he said. "Sometimes it gets a little noisy on weekends. Someone will start a party out front of their place and it will spread. But it's a good place to live," he said starting to laugh as if to be thinking about it.

"It sounds like I will like it here then," I said joining in with the laughter.

Anna came over and wrapped herself around my legs. She looked up at me and meowed.

I picked her up. "This is Anna my best friend," I said as she meowed hello and put her paw out toward Bobby as if to shake hands.

He took her paw gave a slight bow and said, " Glad to meet you Anna." laughed even harder. "Well, I had better get back to the store.

"Good to meet you and I will be seeing you around. Have fun. Bye," I said as he left.

I closed the door and went to put the things away that were in the boxes.

Anna came in a jumped onto the counter putting her nose into one of the boxes.

"Yes, I got you some food too. I got food for a few days. Plus paper towels and paper plates and plastic ware for the next few days. By then I hope to have found some real dished and silverware and a couple of glasses. Oh, and I picked up an application for the café down the street. Maybe I can go to work there and I can get home faster and it will save on transportation cost," I said laughing. "And here is a small radio until I can find a cheap TV. I was told of a thrift store a few blocks away. I will check them out later," I added as I took a small pair of scissors from the box and started cutting the shelf paper to fit the cabinet shelves.

Anna soon got bored and jumped down trotted over to the couch and laid down.

"Oh no," I almost shouted. "I forgot to get pillows while I was out. I will right back," I said grabbing my jacket and racing out the door.

'I hope they are still open,' I thought almost running the few blocks to Grosemen's Department store.

They were just getting ready to close the door as I ran up. "I just need two pillows, please," I said as I hurried through the doors.

I grabbed the first ones I came across and hurried to pay for them. I didn't want to hold them up from closing any longer than I had to.

"I'm sorry I forgot to get these earlier

when I bought the bed, couch and the rest of the bedding earlier," I said apologizing for keeping them late.

"Oh,, this is not a problem. No need to worry," the young lady said as she handed me my change.

"Thank you again for helping me," I said as I took the pillows and headed for the door.

"Bye and thanks," I said to the young man as the door, who was waiting with the keys in his hand.

It didn't take me long to get back home. 'I feel so lucky to have moved into a nice place to live and pretty much everything I need is within a few blocks of my apartment.'

I hadn't noticed it before, but there was a payphone hanging on the wall at the top of the stairs on the second floor. 'Oh, this is nice. I can come here and call Nell and Jack later tonight. No, I need to call them soon. I almost forgot they are later than I am now.

"Hi Anna, here are the pillows," I said as I opened the door.

I tossed the pillows on the bed and picked up Anna. "Let's go make a couple of phone calls," I said as we walked out the door with it locking behind me.

"Hello Nell, I'm here and the apartment is larger than I thought," I said as Nell picked up the phone.

"Good how was your trip?" she asked.

"It went real good. I even sold a pencil

sketch I made while on the bus. And Anna didn't seem to mind the carrier too much. She got out anytime there was a short layover or meal break," I said.

"Meow, Meow," Anna said pawing the phone.

Anna wants to say hi," I said putting the phone closer to her.

"Hi Anna, I hear you are doing pretty good. Do you like your new home?" Nell asked.

"Meeooow," she said.

"I think that is she's not sure yet. She did claim one end of the couch already, but I think that may be because she has her blanket on it," I said laughing.

"Did the place come with any furniture?" Nell asked.

"No, but there is a department store is a very short distance from the and they delivered the bed and the couch earlier today," I replied.

"Good, Well I have an early day tomorrow at work. They are upgrading things in the office," Nell said. "But keep me up on everything that happened. Love you," she added.

"Love you too, goodnight," I said just before hanging up.

"Are you ready to call Jack with me?" I asked looking at Anna.

"Meow," she said quickly.

"It's ringed four times now. I will let it ring a few more before I hang up. They may be working on a time thing," I said without thinking.

Anna meowed softly.

"I know, I know," I said

Jack answered the phone, "Hello?"

"Jack I am so glad you answered the phone. I wanted to talk to you before it got too late," I said.

"Rita my love, how did the trip go? Are you and Anna ok? Where are you calling from?" he said firing off questions faster than I could answer them.

"The trip went great. I even sold a pencil sketch while on the bus. I am calling from the hallway of the apartment house where I am living now. The apartment is set up differently than the one I had there and I think it may be a little bit larger. This is a good place to live. The neighborhood has everything a person would need. There is a grocery store, and department store and café within a few blocks and I heard that the launder mat is the next block over. I got a job app today from the café up the street. I hope to get a job there," I said. "I miss you a lot," I added.

"Well I am saving now and then maybe I can get enough time off to come and see you," he said

"Oh that would be great," I said quickly.

"What are you going to do tonight?" he asked.

"Well, we have a couch and a bed. Oh,

and I managed to find a small radio earlier today. We don't have a TV yet but I have a book. So I guess I will be reading out loud to Anna tonight," I said.

"How is our girl," he asked.

"She is right here with me. You want to say hi to her?" I asked.

"Yes put the phone to her. Hi Anna, How are you doing baby girl?" he asked.

She put her paw on the phone and meowed a long sad meow into the receiver.

"I think she misses you too," I said

"I miss both of you. But like I said I am saving now to come see you. I just don't know when I will get enough time. I still have to tell my boss all that has been going on with us and our plans," he explained.

"I love you so much but I better let you go so you can finish whatever project you were working on," I said.

"Oh true, I should get back to work. Please call about this time tomorrow night," he said. "I love and miss you. Good night love," he said before hanging up.

"Well let's get back upstairs," I said hanging up the phone. "I need to make out that application for work. That way I can take it in tomorrow morning earl," I said as we went up the stairs.

We settled in for the rest of the night. We listened to the radio for a little while then I read to Anna, then we crawled into bed and fell asleep fast I guess because the next thingI knew the sun was shining strongly through our bare windows. I hadn't bothered to hand anything over the windows last night because we had the roof apartment and there was only one building even with us and it was on the side without windows.

"I was thinking Anna. Since we live high enough that no one can see into our windows. Maybe we can just put curtains on the lower half of the windows, except for the windows facing the common space out back," I said talking to Anna.

"Meow," she said which I took as agreeing with a chuckle.

"You are such a good girl. Let eat then I need to get this job app to the café," I said motioning towards the kitchen.

"Food for you and eggs and toast for me," I said putting her food near the stove like it had been in our old apartment.

I soon put my paper plate into the trash and grabbed my jacket and the job app. "See you later. Now you be a good girl while I am gone and I will get back as soon as I have everything taken care of," I said closing the door behind me and making sure it was locked.

I hurried down the street to the café. Handed in my application and made an appointment to talk to the boss for the interview. Then I needed to take care of all the other things the apartment needed to make it like a home.

I went through a few of the thrift and second-hand stores in my area and managed

to find just about everything I needed. I
made arrangements for the TV to be
delivered along with the dresser, a kitchen
table, and two chairs. I could carry the
curtains and the other box of things I found
and decided to buy. I just needed to get it all
back home before the delivery persons got
there.

"Hi Anna, I'm home," I said coming
through the door and putting my jacket on
the couch.

Anna came running from the bed
meowing as she ran.

"Did you have fun today?" I ask
petting her as she jumped up onto the couch.

"I have been all over this side of town
I think. But I think I got everything we could
want or need for a long while," I said petting
Anna and resting at the same time as I pulled
off my shoes.

Just then there was a knock on the
door. I gathered up Anna and we went to see
who it was. "Who is it?" I asked through the
door.

"Delivery for Nate's Thrift goods,"
came the answer.

"Just a minute," I said as I unlocked
the door.

"We have your TV and four other
boxes, a coffee table, and a dresser. Where do
you want it all?" This tall man with a scruffy
looking beard and a large grin asked.

"Well the dresser goes over there, the
coffee table goes in front of the couch and the

TV can go on it. And the boxes can go on the dresser," I said.

Just as I finished saying where I wanted everything, two other guys barged through the door totting the dresser with the two boxes on it. Another guy came walking through the door with the TV after the taller guy with the beard put down the coffee table.

The other guys put everything where I asked and walked out of the apartment but the taller guy said, "You may need an extending cord if you plan to have the TV there," he said.

"Oh, why is that?" I asked curious as to what he would say.

"The plus on this wall only works with the light switch," he offered.

"Oh?" I said.

"Yeah, I use to live here and that plug only works when the light is on," he said. "I plugged in a night light there so when I came home at night I could turn it on and see where I was going," he laughed. "Well enjoy. Good-bye," He added as he walked out the door.

"Thank you and bye," I said closing the door behind him.

"Miss Rita!" came a muffled voice through the door. "Miss Rita Stolks!" it called again.

I looked at Anna. "That is strange, no one knocked."

Chapter Sixteen

I opened the door slowly to see who was calling me. I had Anna in my arms as I stepped out into the short hallway but no one was there.

"Miss Rita! Hello?" came the voice again.

I walked to the edge of the stairs leading to my apartment. Johnny, Miss Beca's grandson was below me at the foot of the stairs.

"Rita, I forgot to tell you if you want phone calls you need to have your name on the board so everyone knows where to find you.

I walked down the stairs to see what he was talking about. And sure enough just slightly above and beside the phone hanging on the way was a message board with a place for each apartment and who lived there, so when someone calls here for someone they will know where to find them.

"That is real nice. Thank you," I said

while pitting my name in the area provided next to my apt number.

"You're welcome. Grandmamma said you were looking for work and I got to thinking that if you got a call and no one knew where to find you, that you would miss the job," he said.

"Good thinking Johnny. Thank you," I said as he walked back down the stairs.

I went back upstairs, put Anna down and moved the coffee table away from the couch so the TV wouldn't be so close and it could be plugged into the other socket without me tripping over it.

Then there were the boxes to unpack. Anna had already found them. She already had half of her body in one of the boxes.

"What are you doing baby girl?" I ask laughing. "Are you going to help me unpack?"

She pulled her head out of the box with a string in her mouth.

"What did you find?" I asked opening the box to find a few other things that I didn't buy. One was a small stuffed animal with a string and bell tied to it. And there was a small fuzzy ball.

"Well it looks like someone was thinking of you," I said while handing her to toys and thinking back to the conversation 'one of the clerks had with me. We got to talking about our pets. I mentioned I had a cat.'

Anna proudly took the stuffed animal

and pranced over to the couch and snuggled up to it.

I went over and turned on the TV and flipped the antenna till I got a picture. "Oh good, we can get a few channels like this," I said looking over at Anna.

Then I went back to unpacking the two boxes. I had bought a few pots, pans and cooking and utensils. I took them to the kitchen then went back for the few plates, glasses, a couple of mixing and cereal bowls. I even managed to find silverware and a few good knives at the thrift store. I found my new toaster in the other box, along with a small blender.

"Oh, my goodness girl time went by faster than I thought. It's already time for dinner," I said. "I guess I had better feed us before we go to bed. I think I am going to do an easy dinner tonight," I said looking over at Anna.

"Meow," she said looking up from her new baby. She stood up stretch the ran into the kitchen.

"Oh, here you go baby," I said putting her food in her bowl.

I opened a can of soup for myself and sat down at the table to eat. Anna soon joined me at the table for a few cracker crumbs. "Now we are home. Right girl?" I said giving her a little taste of my soup.

"Meow," she agreed.

After dinner, we settled in and watched a little TV before going to bed. "I will be going out tomorrow to look for more work and maybe looking over a few blocks of Clay street for my art teacher, Master Bastrono," I said with Anna's full attention.

"Meow," she said then went back to laying her head on her little stuffed animal.

"Time for bed baby," I said walking towards what I now considered the bedroom.

Anna bounced off the couch with her new baby in her mouth and ran to the bed, jumped and landed on her pillow.

Laughing. "You're are so funny baby girl. As she curled up I turned off the lights and said "Goodnight baby,"

It didn't take like before the sun came screaming through the bedroom window and warming up the room. Needless to say, I hadn't put the curtains up yet.

"We had better get up and start the morning girl. First breakfast then to get dressed and I go job and teacher hunting while you play and watch TV," I said climbing out of bed.

Soon I found myself telling Anna to be a good girl while closing the apartment door and going down the stairs to the second floor.

The phone rang just as I pasted. I stopped long enough to answer it.

"Hello?" I said.

"Is Rita Stolks there?" came a lady's voice on the other end.

"Yes, I am Rita," I said.

"Oh good, this is Shela at Dale's Café.
Dale would like to meet with you tomorrow at 2 pm. Can I tell him you will be here?" she inquired.

"Yes mam, and thank you. I will be there at 2 pm tomorrow," I said.

"Good, see you tomorrow then," she said then hung up.

'Wow, I have a job interview tomorrow,' I thought sort of singing it in my head as I finished going down the stairs to the street.

I stopped in at Beca's apartment.

"Miss Beca," I said while knocking on the door.

"Yes dear, can I help you?" she asked as she opened the door.

"Yes mam, do you know what bus I need to take to get to Clay street?" I asked.

"Yes, easier yet, Catch the number ten across the street and ask the driver. He can tell you better than me," she answered with a big smile.

As I waited at the bus stop I saw a couple of people walk by talking on portable telephones.

'I wound where they are getting those phones and how much they are,' I thought as the bus pulled up. I looked at it to make sure it was the number ten I needed.

"Hello, can you tell me how to get to Clay Street?" I asked the bus driver.

"What part of Clay Street are you looking for?" he asked.

"I'm not real sure. I am looking for an art studio and a special teacher. So maybe I need to start at one end and work my way through to the other end," I explained.

"I think I understand. Well, have a seat and I can let you know where you need to get off and what but to catch," he said.

"Okay, thanks," I said as I sat down across from him. 'It's a good thing I have a lot of change in my pockets for the busses today.' I thought.

I watched while the building and street seem to fly by. Soon the driver caught my attention. "Miss you need to take this transfer and catch the number thirteen Clay St bus. It will take you the beginning of Clay Street like you wanted," he said with a big smile.

"Thank you, When is your last run back to when I caught you?" I asked before getting off the bus.

'I will be across the street over there at four-thirty, it you want to ride back with me. My name is Mike. What's your name?" he asked

"Rita," I said with a chuckle.

"The other bus will be here in a few. Bye for now," he said as I turned to go to the other bus stop.

After crossing the street I noticed the street sign. I was at the beginning of Clay Street already. So I decided to start walking and checking out the shops as I went.

After walking for a few hours I started

feeling hungry and spotted a sign that said "Burger Stop" 'cool I can get a burger and maybe a shake' I thought as I walked through the doors.

I sat down at one of the tables and was soon waited on. After eating I went to pay for it and decided to ask if there was an art studio anywhere close to them.

I was told none that any of them knew about. So I left and started my hunt again.

I made it to the two thousandth block before I looked at my watch. "Time is getting away and I may be able to cover maybe one more block before I need to catch the bus back to where Mike let me off," I though softly but aloud to myself.

I spotted what looked like it may be an art studio, but the bus was coming and I wasn't sure when the next one would run. So I figured I had better catch this one and not take the chance today of missing Mike on the way home. I can always start here next chance I get.

I ran across the street at the light and got to the bus stop just in time to catch it.

"Hi, how early do you start running tomorrow?" I asked the driver as I got on.

"I start at 6 am. Are you going to start ride often?" he asked.

"There is a good possibility, yes," I answered. "My name is Rita and I am looking for a special art studio," I explained.

"Well my name is Turner and I will start paying more attention then. And maybe together we can find your special studio," he laughed as I put the money in the farebox. I sat down across from him.

"I need to catch the number ten back home," I explained.

"I can let you know when to get off and where to catch it," he said

"Thanks," I said as I started to watch the streets fly by.

It wasn't long before Turner broke into my thoughts. "Here you are. You need to catch number ten across the street on that corner," he said pointing across from where I got off the bus earlier.

"Thank you, see you tomorrow. I didn't find the studio I was looking for today," I said as I got off the bus.

The lights were right for me to cross right away and it was a good thing too. I spotted the number ten just a block away.

"Hi Rita," said Mike as I got on. "Back so soon?" he laughed.

"Hi Mike, yes but I will cover a little more of Clay street tomorrow morning. Then I have to be back home by noon," I explained as I sat down across from him.

"I'm sure you will find what you are looking for soon," Mike encouraged with a chuckle.

"I'm sure too," I said with a big smile as I sat back and waited for my stop to come up.

Soon I recognized my area. So I reached up to pull the cord but was stopped by Mike. "I know, I'm stopping. See I remembered your stop," he laughed.

I joined in the laughter as I got off the bus. "See you tomorrow," I said waving goodbye.

I opened the door of my new place. "Did you miss me pretty girl," I said as I walked through the door.

She jumped off the bed and ran straight past me to the kitchen.

"Oh is that what all of this about," I laughed. "You hungry baby girl?" I asked.

Meooow," came the answer.

"Me too. But first I need to get these shoes off, then we can eat. I bought hotdogs yesterday and I have a bag of chips.

I hurried over to the couch, pulled off my shoes and jacket then turned the channel on the TV on my way back to the kitchen.

Soon we were both sitting on the couch eating our hotdogs and enjoying a TV program and each other's company.

We watched a little more TV then we went to bed, I laid there and read a little more of my book before falling asleep. Anna curled up right away and was asleep before me.

Anna woke me up with the sun shining on the bed. I looked at my watch and it was almost eight o'clock. "Oh my! Thanks baby girl for waking me up," I said getting up and getting dressed quickly.

She sat on the floor watching me rush around while tilting her head from one side to the other seeming a little confused as to why I was moving so fast.

"Don't worry, we are going to eat before I need to catch the bus," I said while going to the kitchen.

She was on my heels and meowing the whole way. "I will make sure to put down enough food to keep you until I get home. Here is your breakfast," I said putting her dish on the floor and filling the other with milk. I sat down and had a bowl of cereal.

I only had a few minutes before Mike's bus would be heading towards Clay St and I wanted to get in a couple my blocks before noon that way I can be back in time for my job interview.

"Anna, this food is for later. So if you eat it now you may get hungry before I get home. So don't eat it right away. Okay?" I said patting her. I"I need to leave so I will see you later," I said grabbing my jacket and locking the door on my way out.

I had just enough time to get to the bus stop before Mike came by.

I ran the last half block and got to the stop just a Mike pulled up to it. I had to laugh, it reminded me of meeting George in the mornings for work.

"You seem happy this morning. Did you find what you were looking for?" Mike questioned as I got on the bus and dropped the exact change in the fare box.

"No just remembering something that use to happen quite often," I said laughing as

I sat down across from him.

"Ready to go hunting again today?" he asked.

"Yes I am. And my fingers are cross with the hope of finding it today," I said as the bus lunged forward to make the light.

"I will see you in about two hours," I said getting off the bus.

"Hopefully with some good news," Mike said as I got off.

"Bye," I said laughing even more.

I hurried over to the other corner and caught up with Turner's bus the number thirteen Clay St.

"Hi Turner, I'm back," I said as I got on the bus. I need to get off where you picked me up yesterday," I announced while laughing.

"You seem real happy this morning," he said. "Does Rita have a secret?" he asked glancing over at me at the next stop.

"Nope, just a good feeling about today," I said with a big grin.

"I need to get off in the next block," I said as I stood up and held onto the front pole attached to the seat I had been sitting in.

"Ok, But tell me what all of this is about later on your way home ok?" he questioned.

"Okay deal," I laughed while getting off the bus.

I had only looked for about half a block when I saw what could be a small studio with one painting in the window.

Above the door was the numbers 1922.
I took a deep breath and walked through the
door slowly hoping I had found my teacher.
Then looked at my watch.

Chapter Seventeen

The sun came through the front window just enough that you could see pretty good for the first few feet. I stood still hoping that my eyes would adjust to the dimmer areas of the room. Soon I could see a little better. There were a few painting hanging on the walls with small lights over each one. With the rest of the room dimmed the small lighted areas drew in your attention.

I wondered over and was looking at a few when I felt this hand out of the darkness grab hold of my shoulder. I jumped with the suddenness of the touch. I turned to see who it was.

"Rita, my dear you found me. I am so happy you are here," came the voice from the shadows.

Then he stepped into the light of one of the paintings. "Master Bastrono," I said sounding surprised. "You are here," I said turning to face him. "How do you know my name?" I asked.

"You told me some years ago when I first met you. Did you forget? You were going to come back for more lessons but you disappeared shortly after we started your course," he said looking strangely at me. "Are you ready to resume what I was teaching you?" he questioned.

"Yes, but I don't have long to talk today. I have to get back for a job interview. But I have about half an hour," I explained.

"I can use your help around here," he said looking around his store. "Come let me show you the rest of my place. I have a few students that I have been teaching but none of them has your talent. But I wouldn't tell them," he said with a chuckle.

"I have been teaching myself a few things here and there for a while now," I said walking through the heavy drapes he had parted.

The back part of his studio was built like a terrarium with a lot of skylights. The sun was shining fully in all the areas where students were painting.

"So when can you start your studies again. I won't charge for teaching you. You can help me around here in exchange. How does that sound?" he asked with a smile.

"That sounds real good. I like that idea. But I'm not sure what hours I will be working," I agreed.

"Well, when you find out you can let me know. I live in the back so you can drop by any time. We can work around whatever hours you need to work your job," he offered.

"That sounds like a good deal," I said looking at my watch. "I have an appointment that I need to get back for. But I will be back now that I know where you are," I said walking back out to the front of the store with him.

As I walked back down the street to the bus stop I couldn't help but think that he did look real close to the Master Bastrono that showed up at my work back home. But there were some minor differences. He seemed a little taller than he did in my apartment that day and his grip seemed gentler today

Turner got to the bus stop at the same time I got there. "You look a little preoccupied," he said as I got on the bus in almost a daze.

Then I realized he was talking to me. "Oh, what? Sorry I was in deep thought," I said while putting my coins in the box.

"You looked distracted as you got on the bus," I said.

"Oh, I found my art teacher," I said and just made a deal with him for a trade," I explained.

"Oh, then that explained a lot," he said while laughing.

I joined the laughter and sat down in my usual place.

So I was back and my starting point with Turner and was waiting for Mike to show up so I could get back in time to rest for a few minutes before the job interview.

I had just sat down on the bench when Mike drove up.

"Waiting long?" he asked as I got on the bus.

"No I had pretty much just got here," I answered while handing him my transfer.

"Did you find the shop you were looking for?" asked Mike.

"Yes and got the deal I was hoping for. Now I'm headed for home so I can get ready for a job interview," I explained.

"Are you an artist?" Mike asked glancing over at me while waiting on a passenger to get off the bus.

"Yes, I guess I can call myself an artist. I have sold a few paintings," I said with a smile. "My stop is next. See you sometime tomorrow," I said standing up in preparation for getting off.

"Yes, later Rita," Mike called out as I took the last step from the bus.

I waved and walked toward Miss Beca's apartment house.

I ran up the stairs. I had about an hour and a half to spend with Anna before the appointment at Dales Café.

"Hey baby girl, guess what," I said as I closed the door behind me.

She jumped off the couch to meet me and wrapped her tail around my leg to greet me.

"I found my art teacher, the real one

not the future one. I don't think I have to worry about the future one anymore, he's been bands from time travel," I said looking down at her.

We walked into the kitchen together. "I see you sort of waited for me before you ate all of the food in your bowl. Good girl. You are such a good friend," I said picking her up and giving her some loving hugs and scratches.

"I'm not going to add anything to your bowl yet but I should be back in about one and a half hours and we can eat dinner then. Okay?" I said while putting her down.

"Meoow," she said as sort of why.

"I have to go see about this job so we can keep eating," I explained.

She gave me a long loud purr as she walked back over and hopped up onto the couch and laid down.

"I will be back sooner I hope. Maybe I can start work tomorrow," I said as I walked out the door and closing it behind me.

I feel lucky at this point that Dale's Café isn't very far from my apartment and it would be a convenient place to work.

As I walked through the café door Sue recognized me. She gave me the application.

"Rita, just on time Shela, Dale's wife is in the office waiting for you. Right back there," she said smiling as she pointing down a short hallway.

"Thanks," I said giving her a silent thanks as I walked by.

As I got to the office door Shela looked up. "You're the one I called the other day. Rita Stolks?"

"Yes mam," I answered as I fully entered the room.

"Please sit," she said as she looked at my app for a few minutes. Then looking up she asked, "What hours can you work?

"Any hours will be fine," I said hoping to leave the time up to her.

"Are you a night person of early morning?" she asked.

"I have worked all hours and none give me a problem," I answered quickly. "I am willing to work any shift you need me on," I added.

"Good. Can you start tonight? It will be a short shift but it will give you a chance to see how things are done here. Can you be back here at eight o'clock? We close at eleven but then there is cleanup which usually takes a little over an hour," she explained.

"Yes mam, eight o'clock it is. I will be here. Thank you," I said standing and offering my hand.

We shock hands on the deal and I hurried home to tell Anna.

Anna! Guess what, I got the job. I will fix us something to eat then I will need to change clothes so I can go to work tonight. But I should be home a little after midnight.

Work went great and it didn't take long before I know where everything was and had learned the routines of pretty much every shrift. After a couple of weeks, I was given a regular shift. I made friends with all of the regular customers and it's funny, out of all of them there was only a couple that sat in a different place every time they came in.

I called Sam and Julie our explorers, they like ordering something different every time but I had never seen them together.

About three weeks had gone by and I really needed to call Nell. I called and talked to Jack about every other night. But I hadn't taken the time to call Nell as often as I wanted to. But that that I was on a regular shift I was able to coordinate my time a little better.

"Nell? Hey sorry I haven't called more often. I got a job and have had crazy hours. My new boss what to make sure that I knew all of the routines just in case she needed me in some other time slot," I explained.

"I was beginning to wonder if you had forgotten all of us here," she said laughing. I talked to Charlie the other day, he is doing good. They are expecting a baby in about six months. And Sandy got married. Oh, and I slipped on the ice and I'm in a cast," she said.

Oh no, how bad was the break?" I asked.

"Not too bad. I have a walking case so I am hobbling to work and everywhere I need to be. You know nothing slows us down," she laughed.

"I know, it good to hear your voice. Anna is doing good. The new apartment seems more like home now I finally got the curtains up and few rugs on the floor. We are on the top floor so our heating bill is low. Well, I wanted to touch base with you before I went to bed. I was changed to the early shirt this week, which is great because I did find Master Bastrono and I am helping to clean his studio in exchange for lessons and painting supplies. There is a storage closet in the basement here that I can keep my painting in. Ok, well good night. I'll talk to you soon. Goodbye," I said.

"Later sleep good, bye," Nell said then I hear the click of her hanging up the phone.

I went back upstairs and Anna was already one her pillow and I quickly change and got in bed. It must have only taken a few minutes to fall asleep because the next thing I knew, the alarm was going off and Anna was meowing as loud as she could to wake me up.

"Wow girl, I must have been more tired than I thought. What happened to the night? I don't think I even had a dream last night," I said to Anna as we went to the kitchen.

I looked at the clock again to see how much time I had for breakfast.

"I think I have enough time for us to have scrambled eggs this morning," I said looking for Anna's approval.

She jumped onto the kitchen chair and "Meowed" loudly.

"Ok baby girl, I can hear you clearly.

I'm awake," I said laughing as I cracked the eggs and started them cooking.

Time flew and I had to get dressed and get to work.

"I left food and water in your bowls. Try to make it last today. I will be going to the studio after work today so I will be home for dinner," I said giving Anna another hug before putting her down and locking the door behind me.

After work, I had to wait about fifteen minutes for the bus. I figured I would give Jack a quick call. I miss hearing his voice.

"Hello?" Jack said.

"Hi honey, it's me," I said with a chuckle.

"Me who?" he asked laughing.

"Being a comic today hey?" I said. I had a few minutes before the bus takes me to the studio and I figured I would call and talk to you for that little bit," I said.

"I love hearing from you anytime you call. You know that. I wish I could be there. It sounds like you have been making good strides on your paintings according to what you told me yesterday," he said.

"Yes but not quite as much as I would like. But I have been learning a few new things," I said. "Oops, here comes the bus. Gota go. Love you. Talk to you more later. Bye," I said hanging up and running for the bus stop.

"Hi Mike, how's your day been?" I asked as I sat down across from him.

"Going well, today, I haven't had to throw anyone off yet," he said laughing.

Well, I hope you don't have too," I said joining him in laughter.

"Going to the studio today I suppose?" he asked.

"Yep and will see you again on my way home," I said.

"Most likely, I work till ten tonight," he said. "Well here you go," he added.

"That was quick, see you later," I said while getting off the bus.

Turner was just stopping for the light which gave me a chance to get to him before he could leave.

"I see how this is. Catching me at a light so I can't get away," he said laughing.

"You know you would have waited for me," I said laughing.

"Sure I always wait for my regulars," he said taking my transfer just before I sat down behind him this time.

I sat with my head in a position so I would miss my stop.

"Okay missy. Off you go," Turner said stopping the bus.

"Thanks. See you later," I said getting off the bus.

As I walked across the street to the studio I noticed that there was a gym on the corner. 'Now that is an idea. I wonder how much they charge for memberships,' I thought. 'I'm going to go find out,' I thought as I opened the door.

"Hello, can I help you? Sow you around?" the young lady behind the counter said.

"Yes, thank you. How much does it cost?" I asked.

"It depends on what level of service you want," she said. "If you just want to work out it's $10 a month, spas and pool cost a little more. That runs from $25 to $50 a month," she added.

"I think I would like the pool," I said looking around. I could see the pool through the windows that divided it from the rest of the equipment.

"Then you want the $25 package," she said pulling out the paperwork from under her counter.

"Thank you, I will bring them back later today," I said taking them from her. "Right now I have to go to work," I said as I turned to leave.

"Okay, bye," she said with a wave.

Master Bastrono, I'm here," I said announcing myself as I walked through the doorway of the back room.

"Good, Good, You can start over there and after that get set up for your lesson. I have a challenge for you today." he announced.

"Okay," I said as I went to work clearing some of the spaces that had been left a mess. 'Maybe I will learn some of what my future self-learned today,' I thought. "Okay, I am ready," I said.

He was busy with another student. "I will be there in a few minutes. Paint the whole canvas a medium gray color while you are waiting," he instructed.

"Okay," I said while mixing the paints to set up with the right color.

He came over and worked with me for about an hour after his other student had left. I learned a little but it wasn't what I expected. I said good night for the evening and left. I was due back tomorrow at the same time, hoping to learn something that would inspire me.

I walked into the gym and hand the young lady the papers she had given to me earlier along with a check for the month.

I got a chance to work out a little them I checked out the pool. With the fee that I paid I was assigned a locker and given the combination to it.

On the way home I took to memorizing the combination. Said good night to Turner and Mike and walked up the stairs to Anna.

When I opened the door, she was sitting right in front of me as if to scold me for being later than she thought I should have been."Meeoow," she said.

"Sorry baby girl. I know time got away from me, but I'm home now and I see you ate your dinner. But I bet you would like to have something more. Right?" I questioned.

With that she ran to the kitchen. "Ok, I'm on my way," I said pulling off my jacket and tossing it on the couch. "I'm thinking of fixing something easy tonight. It's been a long day," I said getting out some leftovers and popping them into the microwave.

When the bell rang she had her tail wrapped around my legs and was underfoot. "Give me a little room to cool this down. You can't have it this hot. It would make you an owie mouth. Go sit down and I will give you some in a minute," I said, taking it to the counter.

I took out a few spoonful's and put them in her dish as I blew on them to cool them down. Then I stuck my pinky finger in the middle to make sure it wasn't too hot for her. "Okay, here you go," I said placing her dish on the floor next to her water bowl. And I sat down to eat my portion.

"Are you ready for a little TV then bed?" I asked looking over at her licking the last of her dish.

"Meow," she said while prancing over to the couch.

"Well, okay then. What shall we watch? Cowboys, race cars, or news? Not much of a choice tonight, is there girl?" I asked. "Race cars? They look more interesting don't you think?" I asked as I turned it to racing.

She went over and patted the screen then came back and jumped onto the couch and laid down.

"Good choice, I agree," I said as we say back and watched them go faster and faster.

Soon it was over. "Time for bed baby girl. Come on," I said, motioning toward the bed as I got up and headed in that direction.

She was on her pillow by the time I got into bed. "Good night pretty girl," I said turning off the lamp.

I woke up early with Anna in my face with her nose to mine as my alarm went off. "You know when it is time to get up, I think better than the clock," I said laughing. "You make my day Baby girl," I said picking her up, and petting her while we went to the kitchen.

"I'm making oatmeal and scrambled eggs this morning. And I know you like your eggs but I think we will give you a little oatmeal mixed in this morning. It will help fill you up till I can get home to feed you again. I may be late again tonight," I explained.

"Meow, meow," she said jumping onto her chair.

"I know, some milk. I hadn't forgotten. It will be beside you water bowl," I informed her.

I ate and got dress, gave Anna a little more loving and said goodbye and telling her to be a good girl as usual before locking the door behind me.

This routine went on for weeks changing only a few hours here and there. It was starting to be a habit. I could see that Anna was starting to get a little annoyed at not getting out of the house. When we lived in New York she would follow me to the laundry mat and grocery store but here I hadn't really let her out except on the rook for a few minutes here and there. It was time to put a leash on her and let her go to MaBell's Laundromat, after all, it was just around the block. There were no streets to cross. I connected her leash to the wheeled basking I had my clothes in that way she could go with me, but most of the time she was in the basket where she could see everything.

"Okay all done we are ready to go home," I said while loading everything into my rather large backpack.

Soon we were back in the apartment house and she was leading the way up the stairs to our apartment. "Good girl you remembered where you lived," I said opening the door.

She ran straight to the couch and cuddled up with her favorite stuffed toy.

I started taking her with me to a few places that were close to our apartment but on the same block. I didn't want her crossing the streets if she was to get out on her own. The streets here were a little wider than where we use to live and seemed busier.

Soon I was put on the evening shift, so my time was limited as to how long I could stay and help Master Bastrono or go to the gym.

My shifts would change about every

six weeks. Shela said that gives everyone a chance to do the things that they wanted to do or learn. I agree, change can be a good thing. It keeps your life pliable. It's not a good thing for most people to not be able to eccept change.

This would mean that I needed to go take care of Master Bastrono's studio and my lesson earlier in the morning, then go to the gym just before heading home to Anna then off to work. But I seem to have more time with this shift.

Then one day after cleaning and taking my lesson at the studio I decided to go swimming at the gym.

Chapter Eighteen

I had just got into the water and swam one lap when the fire alarm when off. I got out of the pool, got dressed really fast grabbed all of my things and ran out to the front sidewalk. While I was standing out there with everyone else I was taking the things out of my backpack and putting them all back into the right pockets in my jeans and jacket. But my ring was missing. The chain was here but the ring was missing.

The police and fire marshal showed up and said it was a false alarm and everyone could go back into the gym. I went in and reported my ring missing. I gave a detailed description to the policeman that was still at the gym making sure that everything was ok after reporting it to the gym.

I was told they would keep a watch for it but chances were I wouldn't see it again. Things like that disappear in a big city pretty easy. I explained that it was special and that my fiancé was an inventor and well it was a special ring.

"We will keep an eye open for it but you may never see it again," he said before walking away.

Frustrated I headed home before I had to go to work.

"Hi Rita," Turner said. "Heading home so soon? What's up, you look down," he added.

"I was at the gym and someone stole my engagement ring," I said as I sat down.

"Did you report it?" he asked.

"Yes and was told I may never see it again," I said looking down.

"Well keep your fingers crossed. Sometimes things get found and returned," he said trying to lift my spirits. "Here's your stop. See you tomorrow?" he questioned.

"Yes still have a life and things to do," I said as I left the bus with the transfer in hand.

"Hey Rita, you ok? What happened?" Mike asked as I hand him the transfer.

I told him the story and he tried to encourage me to keep positive thoughts. I thanked him as I got off the bus and headed for the apartment.

I was crying by the time I got upstairs.

I opened the door and Anna met me as I took the first step through the door.

I sat down on the couch and cried for a while. I knew I had to call Jack and let him know what my new hours were so he would know when to call me. But I had decided not to tell him about the ring. He didn't need to worry. We could always track in later.

Anna was on my lap trying her best to give me love. Meowing and patting my face as the tears rolled down my cheeks.

I knew I was loved no matter what. But I had decided to keep the loss to myself for the time being and give the police a running chance anyway.

I looked at my watch and it was time to go call Jack.

"I'll be right back. I'm going to call Jack and let him know my hours and then we can eat," I said as I walked out the door.

I had pulled myself together enough to make the call.

The phone rang about six times and no one answered. 'Where could he be? He should be home by now, even if he stepped out to go to the store. Well, I guess I will try after work tonight,' I thought.

A little disappointed I walked by up the stairs to our apartment and started making Anna and I something to eat. I didn't feel very hungry tonight after all that had happened so I pretty much picked at whatever was in the refrigerator but I made sure that Anna what plenty to eat and drink before I had to go to work.

"I will see you a little after midnight baby girl. You are really loved you know that?" I ask giving her a little squeeze before putting her down and locking the door behind me and headed for my shift at the café

Unknown to me Jack had made arrangements to sneak into San Francisco without letting me know as a surprise visit.

I tried calling Jack again after I got off work but still no answer. 'Now that makes me evermore stressed. First my ring and now Jack.' I thought and before I knew what I was doing I was almost shouting "I DON'T WANT TO LOSE ANYTHING ELSE TODAY!" I put my hand over my mouth as soon and I hear my voice. I had been taught better than that. Keep negative things out of your mouth and mind if you can. It can cause trouble. "I will find my ring and Jack and all is good," I said out loud just as loud as I had said the other things.

I kept repeating that all the way home.

Anna cuddled with me all that night.

I woke up the next morning with Anna meowing and walking back and forth across me.

"Ok pretty girl, I'm awake and I'm getting up," I said just as the alarm went off. I had to laugh. "You're a much better alarm and that crazy sounding clock," I said petting her as I brushed my hair.

"Meow," she said following me to the kitchen.

"Yes, I am feeling better this morning. If the police don't find the ring Jack can track it where ever it is," I explained. "Yes, let's eat," I added.

Anna meowed two more times as she jumped onto her chair and watched while I made up something to eat.

"Okay, baby girl there is yours all ready for you and it is cool enough for you to eat," I said as I place her dish on the floor.

"I have to leave for the studio soon and then back here with you for dinner then to work. So I will see you later today," I said petting Anna a few more times before walking out the door heading for the studio.

Jack thought he would catch up with Rita at the café. She had told him the address and the address of the apartment. But instead, he was tracking the ring to a different part of town. At this point, he was feeling a little confused. He was in a taxi telling the driver which way to turn. He had told the taxi that is just wanted to go riding and that he would give him direction as they went. Which the driver was glad to do because fares like this usually gave him a good tip and ran up quite a large bill.

Meanwhile. Jack was getting even more confused. He was lead to one part of town but now he was tracking it across town to another area. Soon he found himself stopped in front of a strange-looking building.

"What building is this?" he asked the driver.

"It's uh, the city morgue sir," he answered slowly.

"The morgue, No this had got to be the wrong address. It's the wrong place. It can't be right. Things don't change that much," Jack was saying out loud.

"I'm sorry sir. What?" asked the driver.

"Never mind, just wait right here for me. I will be out soon. You can leave the meter running if you want. Just wait for me," Jack almost screamed as he got out of the taxi.

"Yes sir, I will be right here," the driver said.

Jack hurried into the building.

There was an older man sitting at a desk. Then a younger man came out of a room next to the desk.

"What's in that room?" Jack asked.

"The young lady we just brought in," the young man said. "Who are you looking for? May I ask?" he inquired.

"A young woman with dark brown hair, about five foot four inches," Jack said describing Rita.

"Then come with me," the young man said leading Jack into the room.

There in front of Jack for a gurney with a body covered by a white sheet.

"Would you like to take a look?" questioned the young man.

Jack hesitated to answer then got enough courage together and say "Yes."

The young man drew back the sheet so that the face of the young woman shown in the harsh lights.

Jack took a deep breath of relief. "It's not the one and I am so glad.

I made a special ring for my fiancé and I invented a tracking device that I placed on the ring.

"Can you describe the ring?" the young man asked.

"Yes, in the gold with a heart on it," Jack said.

The young man went to his desk and pulled out an envelope and then reached inside. "Is this it?" he asked as he pulled his hand out of the envelope.

Jack could see from across the room that it was Rita's ring. "Yes that is the one I bought in New York over a year and a half ago. Yes, can I have it?" he asked.

"I have to make a phone call first and then we will see where it leads us," he explained.

With that, the young man picked up the phone and dialed. "Hello, Police? Yes, can I talk to your person that has the list of stolen items please? Yes I will hold. Yes, I need to know if there was a ring reported stolen? Yes. This is the city morgue and I have a person here that wants to claim the item in question. Yes it has a heart. Okay I have the original owner here in my office. Yes, then take it off your list there and I will sign the paperwork here. Yes, and thank you. Good-bye," the young man said and hung up the phone.

"Here you go," he said handing Jack the ring. "It seems you fiancé reported it stolen from the gym she was at a few days ago," he explained.

"Well thank you so much. I will make sure she gets it back. She doesn't know that I am in town. I wanted to surprise her," Jack explained with a smile.

"Good for you. I hope everything turns out the way you want it to," The young man said as he turned and walked back through the doors.

"Do you need a ride?" the old man asked.

"No I have a taxi waiting, thanks," Jack said while walking out the door to the taxi. "Now please take me to 228 Lauren St," Jack said as he closed the taxi's door.

"Yes sir right away," the driver said.

It didn't take long before he was sitting in front of the apartment house where Rita lived.

He got out and paid the driver generously. Then he walked up the steps and knocked on apartment A. "Miss Beca March?" he asked as Beca answered the door.

"Yes, Can I help you?" she asked.

"Yes, I think you can. Do you know if Rita is home? I'm Jack, Jack Monroe her fiancé. I want to surprise her. I found her ring," he said holding it up for Beca to see.

"She is at work right now, but I don't think she would mind if you waited for her in her apartment. She's told me about you and what you looked like. It's as if I know you already," she said laughing as she led him upstairs.

As Beca opened the door, Jack spotted Anna.

"Anna baby girl, you are a sight for tired eyes," he said stooping over to pick her up.

"Well it seems kitty knows you," Beca said laughing.

"Yes, we are old friends. Thank you Miss Beca March," Jack said.

"Just Ms. Beca. I will leave you two to visit. Good night Jack Monroe," she said with a slight giggle as she turned and started down the stairs.

Jack sat on the couch and kept Anna company for a very long time before they both fell asleep watching TV.

A few hours later Rita unlocked the door and Anna wasn't at the door waiting. Rita turned on the light and saw a person on her couch.

"Who is in my house?" she shouted.

Anna bounced off the couch and came running.

As Jack opened his eyes and sat up he saw Rita and said, "Oh, hi honey. I guess we fell asleep watching TV."

"What, How? I mean, when did you get here?" I asked.

"I got here earlier today and boy what a wild adventure I have had," Jack said.

"Okay well you have to tell me what happened that was so wild today," I said heading for the kitchen after a few hugs and lots of kisses.

Jack sat and told Rita his whole adventure since he left New York till now, over a cup of coffee.

"What a rush," I said after hearing all that had happened. "So where is my ring. It got stolen while I was swimming the other day," I explained.

"Yes, I was told all of that. I have it right here. But so you don't lose it again. How about let go put it on your figure tomorrow?" He asked.

"Wow really? What happed to waiting till your boss says it's okay?" I ask.

"True that. I keep forgetting that I have to wait for them to say okay to things I want to do," he said. "Okay, I guess we will have to wait on them. But we could do our own promises and then not worry about the rest till they say okay. What do you think?" he asked with a big grin.

"Well let me sleep on it," I said laughing. "It's time for bed anyway. You get the couch," I said laughing.

"Really?" Jack exclaimed.

"Only because I have an early morning. We all changed shifts again" I explained. "Wait! How long are you going to be able to stay for?" I asked feeling all excited about his visit.

"I only have a week off work. Then it is back to the routine again. Let me hold you for a while at least till you fall asleep," he begged.

"Well okay but it will be squishy because Anna has her spot already claimed as you can see," I explained.

"Yes, I see that," he said as Anna raised her head off her pillow proudly.

"Maybe I can bring the TV over here and we can watch an old movie or something," Jack suggested.

"Okay if you want," I agreed as he headed over toward the TV.

It was soon sitting at the end of the bed.

Just as he turned the TV back on a sifi movie was starting.

About halfway through it the movie Jack said. "I was thinking. I have enough credits saved that we could live modestly pretty much the rest of our lives on it, if I was to quit my job now. The only problem that may be of a concern is, I would start aging again."

"How fast would you age?" I asked looking into his eyes.

"I have been told that the aging would be about two years for every year that goes by in your time. And in the end, I would the right age for my time. They figure when I'm about eighty years old. But I would still get to keep my health plan they would just pay the doctors in your time. I was thinking about asking them to let me end my contract with them. I would normally be retiring in five years anyway. What do you think?" he asked holding me even closer.

Chapter Nineteen

"Let me think about all of this. You have given me a lot all at once. I want to marry you and the sooner the better, but I have a lot on my plate right now. I mean I just got settled here and I have a new job and I like the people I am working for and I just met my teacher. I'm just getting used to the going back and forth between the job and the studio," I explained.

"I know. And you are holding it altogether real good. I was just thinking that if I was to take my retirement now, our housing would be paid and you could work if you want to and not because you had to and someone would be here with Anna while you were gone. And…" his voice trailed off as Anna raised her head from hearing her name call. "You're okay baby girl, my sweet Anna," Jack said stroking her gently.

"But we hadn't talked about having a family or anything like that," I said sort of leaving it in the air.

"We can do that if that is something you want to do. I would love to have a family, but that is totally your choice. Just loving you is enough for me if you chose that too," he explained.

"How soon? I mean what all needs to be done for us to get married and you to retire?" I asked.

"I just need to ask. But you know they have a station here in San Francisco and if they insist that I need to complete my contract, they can transfer me here," he explained.

"Okay then how long before we would know what they say?" I asked.

"I didn't ask them yet I wanted to see what you thought about the whole situation first," he said.

"Do you have to go back to ask or can you just call them from here?" I asked.

"While you are at work tomorrow I will go into the center here and ask questions. Okay?" he said.

"Yes please, if they transfer you here can we still get married now or do we have to wait till you retire with them? I asked just for curiosity's sake.

"I can give you that answer tomorrow," he said as we settled back to watch the rest of the movie.

Morning came fast and found us holding each other just as we had been watching TV. In fact, the TV was still on and it was news time.

I got up, got dressed and started breakfast. It wasn't long before Anna Jack joined me in the kitchen. We all ate breakfast and I headed off to work. And if all went well Jack planned to go into their travel center to talk to the bosses through their communication system.

By the time I got off work, curiosity got the best of me and I had to see if Jack was home and if he had found out anything.

I ran up the stairs and opened the door to find Anna sitting on the couch watching TV. Jack had managed to find a channel with animal programs. But there was no sign of Jack. I closed the door and checked Anna's food dish. There was still food in it and she had plenty of water. I looked over at her and she was watching every move the ducks on TV were doing. Like a child glued to cartoons. I had to laugh.

"Okay baby girl I will see you later," I said closing the door behind me.

I ran down the stairs so I could be at the bus stop in time to meet Mike. 'Aw, just in time,' I thought as I spotted Mike almost a block away.

"Hi Mike," I said with a big smile on my face.

"You seem mighty happy today," he said as I dropped my change in the fare box.

"Yep. See," I said holding up my hand. "Jack found my ring and we decided it is safer for me to wear it on my hand than around my neck," I announced.

"Is Jack you fiancé?" Mike questioned.

"Yes, and he came in ad surprised me last night. I didn't know he was coming," I said with a giggle.

"That is nice. Are you going to the studio today?" he asked.

"Yep, need to get off at my regular place," I said looking out the window.

"Get ready it is next," he announced.

"Ready set, go," I said standing up near the door as Mike put on the brakes.

He started laughing as I got off and ran to catch Turner waiting across the street at the light.

"Just in time Rita," he said laughing.

I joined the laughter.

"Feeling better today I see," he said.

"Yes, found my ring. So I am happy. Plus my fiancé dropped in on me last night as a surprise," I said.

"Is that a good thing?" Turner questioned.

"Yes, a very good thing. Long-distance is hard and he was in New York. Now he may be able to stay here," I explained as I stood up by the door. "This is my stop coming up."

"Yes, you are right," Turner laughed. "See you later," he added

"Yep, later," I said stepping off the bus.

Master Bastrono was standing at the door of his studio as I walked up.

"My hours were changed again," I

explained.

"Okay, you know what needs to be done. I will be there in a few minutes," he said.

He seemed a little odd today. So when he came back into the shop I asked, "What is happening? Things seem different today," I said looking in his direction.

"I don't know I just feel strange. The vibrations are strange today. Not really sure how to put it into words. I guess like the static electric before a big storm. But the skies are clear," he said as he walked towards the back part of the studio. "Oh, by the way, I stacked all of your painting in that corner over there," he said pointing to the far corner of the studio. "I figured that way they are out of sight of my other students. You are almost a master compared to them and I didn't want them to get discouraged," he explained.

"Ok, I was going to ask if I could use a small area for my art sort of out of the way from everything else," I said smiling.

"Sure then that is your area. I will put a light over there and you can do your painting there, if that is what you want," he said with a chuckle.

"Yes please," I said as I went back to cleaning.

I took my art lesson and put that painting with the others in my corner. Then left for the gym and played there for about thirty minutes. I figured it was about time to catch Turner on his way through.

"Hi Turner, have a good day since I saw you last," I said laughing. he and I both knew it had only been a few hours.

"Sure," he laughed. "On your way home or work?" he asked.

"Home this time," I said sitting down across from him. I liked the front seat because I could watch the building fly by.

"Okay see you tomorrow," I said standing by the door prepared the get off as soon as he stopped.

I spotted Mike across the street and waved so he would see me and wait.

"Another few seconds and you would have had to wait for my next run," Mike said as I gave him my transfer.

"I know that is why I waved at you," I said laughing. "I'm in a hurry tonight," I added.

"Okay hold on," he said as he hurried through the light.

I ran up the stairs and Jack met me at the door, reached out and gave me a hug right off, then a kiss before I could get through the door.

"How did your day go," he asked.

"It went real good. Something smells good. Did you cook dinner?" I asked.

"No I ordered out and it just came. I ordered it from Lobsing's . I found them three blocks over and they deliver," he said.

"Good, let's eat while it is hot," I said heading for the sink to wash my hands.

I looked down and Anna had already

started. "You must be hungry pretty girl," I said laughing. She was working on a fist-size piece of chicken.

"You are going to spoil her if you're not careful," I laughed while joining Jack at the table.

"I know and she is loving every minute of it," he said laughing.

"So what did your bosses say?" I asked.

"I can transfer here and I can start work on the last day of my vacation. And yes we can get married. But I have to finish my contract with them. So I am going to go back to New York tomorrow and pack up all of the things that I want to keep and send them here. If that is okay with you," he said.

"Yes as long as it fits in this apartment," I said giving him a big smile.

"Well not to worry the furniture isn't mine. So it will all be little stuff," he said.

Good. That will work. We will have to get another dresser. But we have room for that on the other side of the bathroom door," I said with a giggle.

"So we can get married as soon as I get back. If everything goes like I want it to I can be back as soon as the next day," he informed me.

"The next day," I questioned.

"Yes, we have transporters at each time station. So moving from one station to another isn't a problem," he explained. "But you know you can't let anyone know any of this," he added.

"Oh, I know and so does Nell. We learned to keep secrets when we were very young. And both of us a good at it," I stated.

"I know and I trust both of you. Just thought I would throw that in," he said with a cheesy grin.

The next few days went fast. Then there was a knock at the door.

I opened the door and there stood Jack with three large suitcases and a very large backpack.

I motioned for him to come on in and as he moved through the door Nell popped out from behind the backpack.

"Nell!, Wow! I am glad to see you. How long can you stay?" I asked.

"Jack's work gave me a one day pass. I can stay through tomorrow's midafternoon. I get to be her as your witness and bride's maiden," Nell explained.

"Oh, that is so nice. Thank you Jack, for doing that for me," I said turning to give him a big hug.

"How is your leg?" I asked turning to Nell.

"Oh, it's great, the cast comes off next week," he said.

"Kool. I hope you don't mind the couch," I said.

"Jack got me a room in the motel around the corner," she informed me.

"Oh good that will give you more room," I said looking at Jack. "You are full of surprises," I added.

"Yes and you should know," he said pausing for effect.

"Know what? Know what?" I asked in excitement.

"Andrew is her as my best man. Nell and Andrew met last month and the love bug sort of bit them too. But Andrew has a ten year contract to fulfill before he can do anything serious because he travels from one station to another," Jack explained.

"Nell you didn't tell me that. Why didn't you tell me?" I questioned with a big smile.

"I didn't know you knew Andrew until Jack told me on the way here. And Andrew said not to tell anyone about us," she said sheepishly.

"Oh not to worry, it's all in the family," I said laughing.

"It really is. Isn't it?" Nell laughed.

"So, is Max living with you, now that Jack will be here?" I asked remembering that Jack said that Max was Andrew's dog but was staying with Jack.

"Yes, I now have a dog," Nell said proudly.

I had to laugh. "So you know and understand about Max?" I questioned.

"Yes, Andrew filled me in. I like the idea," Nell said proudly. "Well morning will come soon enough and Andrew should be back at the motel by now and I am really tired," she added.

We walked with Nell to her room at the motel and Andrew was there waiting for her.

"Rita, Jack filled me in on all that is happening. You know that you two are breaking new ground for all of us," Andrew said while giving me a hug. "Nell and I plan to follow in your footsteps sort of speak. Well goodnight I have a heavy day tomorrow but I have timed your marriage in so I wouldn't miss it," he added.

Jack and I walked back to our apartment and turned in also. I still have to work tomorrow morning and I think I can get by with just a short time with Master Bastrono. So I can meet everyone at City Hall in time to get dressed in something I will need to buy before showing up there.

When I woke up breakfast was ready.

"Good morning love. I woke up about half an hour ago and decided you needed the extra time to do what you wanted for a few minutes before you take off for work," Jack said reaching out to give me a hug and a morning kiss as he pulled the chair out for me to sit down to eat.

"Wow what a breakfast, pancakes, bacon and eggs," I said while taking the syrup. Thank you," I said looking over at Anna. "Oh aren't you privileged with your slice of ham," I added laughing.

Anna looked up at me and meowed.

After taking my time eating I had to hurry to get to work on time. As I walked through the door Shela met me.

"Stop right there," she said. "You're not working today," she added.

"Am I fired?" I asked feeling almost sick in my stomach.

"No, you're not fired. You're getting married today at three o'clock at City Hall and so you need the time to get a dress and your hair fixed or whatever you want. You're off today. But be here tomorrow. Okay?" Shela said. "Now go," she added with the shooing motion of her hands.

'How did she find out I was getting married today. I hadn't told anyone at work,' I thought as I walked to the bus stop.

"Hi Mike," I said still feeling confused. I put my money in and sat down in the front seat.

"What up?" Mike asked.

"Shela gave me the day off to get married. But I hadn't told anyone at the café I was getting married. How did she know?" I asked

"You live in this community and it only takes one person to say something and within minutes everyone knows. Someone mentioned it to someone else and there it went," he explained. "Don't worry, enjoy your day," he added.

"Ok," I said standing u to get off the bus as soon as the doors opened. Turner was at the light and I would have to run to catch him.

I waved as I ran. I was lucky he seen

me. I got on and handed the transfer to him and sat down.

"Going to the studio today?" he asked.

"Yes for a few minutes. Then I need to find a department store that had nice dresses," I said.

"A nice dress. Let me think. Oh yeah try Barnet's Department Store, it's about three blocks farther down from the studio," he said.

"Okay, thanks. Then what bus do I need to catch to get to city hall?" I asked.

"Catch my going in this same direction and I will let you off where you need to catch the number six bus. They can let you off there," he instructed. "See you soon," he added as I stepped off the bus.

"Thanks," I said giving him a wave.

I walked into Master Bastrono's studio as a policeman walked by me on his way out.

"What happened?" I asked as I got closer to Master Bastrono.

"Really odd," he kept repeating.

"What is?" I asked.

"It seems we had a break-in last night but the only things missing were eight of your ten paintings you had in the corner," he said looking over at me.

"Which ones?" I said running to see which ones had been taken.

"Oh No, all of my best ones," I said. "Well that's not fair," I added.

"Well, I can't worry about that right now. I have to keep going in the right direction," I mumbled to myself.

"What are you saying? I didn't hear you," Master Bastrono said walking up behind me.

"I'm getting married in a few hours and so I will have to worry about this later," I said. I will see you tomorrow. Okay?" I questioned.

"Sure, Sure go get married. I will figure this out. See you tomorrow. Good-bye," he said waving his hand at me.

I went farther down Clay Street hoping to find the store Turner had told me about. 'Oh there it is in the next block,' I thought walking a little faster.

As I walked through the doors I was able to find the dresses right off. The area was well marked. I tried on about five. I'm not too much on wearing dresses. But I did finally find a blouse and a skirt I liked a lot.

After paying for the clothes I spotted their hair salon.

'Maybe I will see if I have enough money left for them to layer my hair,' I thought.

"How much does it cost to have my hair layered?" I asked.

The gal up front looked at my hair and said, "Around $30."

"Okay thank you," I said as I walked away.

'I'll ask Nell to help me with my hair when I get to City Hall. They are bound to have a bathroom there,' I thought while waiting on Turner to come by.

"Well, I see you found a few things. Good," he said as I got on the bus.

I paid the fare and sat down up-front.

"Yes, thanks. How long does it take to get to the street to catch the next bus?" I asked.

"It will take about twenty minutes from here," he answered while watching the traffic.

I looked at my watch, 'it's fifteen minutes after one now and I had to be at City Hall by three and I still needed my hair done and to get dressed. This is going to be so close,' I thought. I could feel my stomach tightening. 'Slow my breathing. Things will work out,' I kept telling myself.

Chapter Twenty

"Rita! Over here," Nell whispered loudly giving a short wave. "Let's get to the bathroom quick. We only have about thirty minutes before the judge will be ready for you. I'm glad you got here when you did," she said. "There what do you think?" Nell asked standing behind me and looking in the mirror.

"I think we did good and we have ten minutes to spare. We did good. Thank you for all of this," I said turning and giving Nell a tearful hug.

"Now do go ruining your makeup," she said. "Pat dry don't rub," she added.

We walked out of the bathroom just in time to see the clerk come out of the doors and motion for all of us to come in.

I hurried and grabbed Jack's hand and we walked in together with Andrew and Nell right behind us.

The ceremony was quick and we all went to eat at a nearby restaurant. Then we went back to our apartment for a peaceful night, Nell and Andrew had one more night at the motel.

We got up very early to see Nell back to the New York station then Andrew, Jack and I all had to go to work.

Time past and I managed to paint a few more paintings that I thought were worth keeping and so I placed them behind the ones that were left behind when the others were taken.

Then one night Master Bastrono's studio was broken into again, but this time not only was the painting taken but Master Bastrono got into a fight with the burglar and got his left arm hurt past repair then the studio was burned to the ground. Master Bastrono was lucky to escape.

The police artist made sketches of the burglar with Master Bastrono's help. He could draw because he had been left-handed. But he did manage to have a good picture drawn and got extra copies of the picture.

He gave me one of the copies and I gave it to Jack who sapped it onto his boss. It didn't take long before the caper was figured out.

Andrew came over for dinner shortly after that and told us what had happened.

"Do you remember when you lived in New York and the future Master Bastrono came by to teach you to paint but then he didn't come back?" Andrew asked me.

"Yes, " I said. "I was told he was caught and they made a ruling that he wasn't allowed to time travel anymore. Right?" I added.

"Yes. But somehow he and a friend decided to come back and get more of your paintings. Then they got in a fight and MB got greedy. So his friend decided to come back earlier and beat him to the paintings. But got the wrong time and the original Master Bastrono got badly hurt before the fire destroyed everything. Anyway they were both caught and chipped with a tracker in the skull where they can't take it out. And the future MB has to deal with the injury his friend did to him in the past." Andrew related.

"Wow, what a story. Well, for me I am glad I don't have to deal with either anymore. Oh, and you know what, the first paintings that were taken? Jack and I found them in my storage locker here in the basement when we went to store a few things. Isn't that funny?" I said laughing with Jack joining me.

"That is," Andrew said joining in the laughter. "Oh and the painting his friend brought back with him were taken and given to your future self. Those paintings can't be sold in our time because the type of paint used has been outlawed. They have lead in them," he added with a hardy chuckle.

After talking a little long Andrew saw me looking at my watch.

"It's been nice and I loved being here and visiting but it is getting late and we all have to work tomorrow. So I am going to say goodnight," he said standing up and grabbing his jacket.

"You know you are welcome anytime you are near or have time off," Jack said, giving him a hug and I managed to get a hug before he opened the door.

"Well you both know where I will be if and when I get time off work," he said.

We both knew he was talking about Nell and we said "Yes," almost in unison and then laughed.

"Bye," I said as we shut the door behind him.

Time fly by and started to gain a little weight. I decided to find out for sure what I thought was happening was for real.

Yep, sure enough, we were having a baby.

Jack came home that night and I had dinner on the table and candles lit.

"What's the occasion?" he asked.

"Well sit down and I will tell you," I said with a big smile. "You remember me telling you that I had been gaining weight?"

"Yes," he answered.

"We are having a baby. And the timing is perfect. You get to retire in two years and that means our child will be grown before you too old to enjoy the time we will all have. And we will be aging at almost the same rate since I now have a four-year jump on you," I said laughing. "Isn't this great?" I asked.

"This is wonderful," he said picking me up off the ground and dancing me around the room with both of us laughing the whole time.

"But you know in reality I will be in my eighties by the time our child is grown," he said looking at me strangely.

"But think of all the knowledge you can teach our child. This is a blessing I know we will both enjoy," I said giving him a big kiss and laughter broke out again.

"Well let's eat. I'm starved," he said as we sat down to dinner.

"I just got to wondering. How much of my history did your bosses let you have? Did you know about our child? I mean did they give you a heads up about the future?" I asked, looking over the table at him.

"No, I wasn't told much about you at all. All I knew when I met you was that you were a good artist and had come back for a vacation. But I knew you were real pretty and honest and I liked what I saw," he said winking at me.

"Really, that is all you knew or know about me?" I ask.

"Well I know a little more about you now than I did then," he said.

Yeah, like what?" I asked.

"I know that you love me no matter how old and ugly I get," he said laughing.

"Eat your dinner," I said joining him in laughter.

Soon the time came for the birth of our little girl and we named her Jessy Ann Monroe.

I went on with my art and Jessy was very smart and earned scholarship after scholarship and was soon in one of the major medical Universities.

We were so proud of her. She decided to be a spine and joint specialist. She had a few ideas of her own as to new ways to handle problems and soon invented a way to take out broken vertebra and replace them with a vertebra that comes in piece and is snapped together in place and the disk in snapped into place without doing any harm to the spinal cord or the nerves.

Time had been slipping by faster than I was keeping track of and I lost Jack and age eighty-four years and I had gotten to the age that I wanted to do things but years were trying to catch me too.

I fell and cracked a vertebra of two and I couldn't get around like I needed to.

Jessy came by to visit and between the two of us, we decided I needed to undergo the procedure she had come up with. So I went for the operation and my back was as good as new. But it had pretty much token all of my savings. So I save as much as I could and borrowed the rest to take the trip I had taken so many years before as Anna May.

On all of my records, the Anna May Stolks was put down as my AKA.

But when I came back from my
vacation I had plenty of money to live the life
that Jack had always wanted for us.

Other Books Written
by
Lauresa Tomlinson

Chapter Books

The Turning Stone
Secretly Special
My Interview With a Fairy
There's an Alien in My Cereal
Crazy Déjà vu
Elaytay's Adventures in Space and Time – (parts 1-3)
We Came to Visit (part One)
We Meet at Last (part Two)
Which Times May be (part Three)

Picture Books
Munchie and Goldie – Most Unlikely Friends
Cats in Charge
Sleepy Time Baby Bear

Other Books
Expressive Tree People
Studies of Life –Poetry
Procrastinator's Hand Book (note book)

More to come…

www.ingramcontent.com/pod-product-compliance
Lightning Source LLC
Chambersburg PA
CBHW070623170726
48291CB00003B/858